THE SLIP GUN CHANGED

Its owner
all the spee
ized weapo
achieve with
modified in
profanity as
killer twirle
the wall, the
sured his le

"Are you all right, Mark?" Ramsbottom inquired.

"Why, sure," the blond giant replied. "And, like I was saying just before we were interrupted, welcome back to Texas, Waxahachie Smith."

"Gracias," Ramsbottom replied. "Only, seeing's how this's the *second* time I've had to stop jaspers trying to kill me since I crossed the New Mexico line, I'm beginning to wonder how come *somebody* doesn't want sweet, lovable, li'l ole me to come back."

List of J. T. Edson *titles in chronological and categorical sequence:*

Ole Devil Hardin series

YOUNG OLE DEVIL
OLE DEVIL AND THE CAPLOCKS
OLE DEVIL AND THE MULE
   TRAIN
OLE DEVIL AT SAN JACINTO
TEXAS FURY

The Civil War series

COMANCHE
THE START OF THE LEGEND
MISSISSIPPI RAIDER
REBEL VEN
THE BIG GUN
UNDER THE STARS AND BARS
THE FASTEST GUN IN TEXAS
A MATTER OF HONOUR
KILL DUSTY FOG!
THE DEVIL GUN
THE COLT AND THE SABRE
THE REBEL SPY
BLOODY BORDER
RENEGADE

The Floating Outfit series

THE YSABEL KID
.44 CALIBRE MAN
A HORSE CALLED MOGOLLON
GOODNIGHT'S DREAM
FROM HIDE AND HORN
SET TEXAS BACK ON HER FEET
THE HIDE AND TALLOW MEN
THE HOODED RIDERS
QUIET TOWN
TRAIL BOSS
WAGONS TO BACKSIGHT
TROUBLED RANGE
SIDEWINDER
RANGELAND HERCULES
McGRAW'S INHERITANCE
THE HALF BREED
WHITE INDIANS
TEXAS KIDNAPPERS

THE WILDCATS
THE BAD BUNCH
THE FAST GUN
CUCHILO
A TOWN CALLED YELLOWDOG
TRIGGER FAST
THE MAKING OF A LAWMAN
THE TROUBLE BUSTERS
DECISION FOR DUSTY FOG
CARDS AND COLTS
THE CODE OF DUSTY FOG
THE GENTLE GIANT
SET A-FOOT
THE LAW OF THE GUN
THE PEACEMAKERS
TO ARMS! TO ARMS! IN DIXIE!
HELL IN THE PALO DURO
GO BACK TO HELL
THE SOUTH WILL RISE AGAIN
THE QUEST FOR BOWIE'S BLADE
THE TEXAS ASSASSIN
BEGUINAGE IS DEAD!
MASTER OF TRIGGERNOMETRY
THE RUSHERS
BUFFALO ARE COMING!
THE FORTUNE HUNTERS
RIO GUNS
GUN WIZARD
THE TEXAN
OLD MOCCASINS ON THE TRAIL
MARK COUNTER'S KIN
THE RIO HONDO KID
OLE DEVIL'S HANDS AND FEET
WACO'S DEBT
THE HARD RIDERS
(   )
THE FLOATING OUTFIT
APACHE RAMPAGE
THE RIO HONDO WAR
THE MAN FROM TEXAS
GUNSMOKE THUNDER
THE SMALL TEXAN
THE TOWN TAMERS
RETURN TO BACKSIGHT

WEDGE COMES TO ARIZONA
ARIZONA RANGE WAR
ARIZONA GUN LAW
(   )

Waco series

WACO'S BADGE
SAGEBRUSH SLEUTH
ARIZONA RANGER
WACO RIDES IN
(   )
THE DRIFTER
DOC LEROY, M.D.
HOUND DOG MAN

Calamity Jane series

TEXAS TRIO
COLD DECK, HOT LEAD
THE BULL WHIP BREED
TROUBLE TRAIL
THE COW THIEVES
THE HIDE AND HORN SALOON
CUT ONE, THEY ALL BLEED
CALAMITY SPELLS TROUBLE
WHITE STALLION, RED MARE
THE REMITTANCE KID
THE WHIP AND THE WAR LANCE
THE BIG HUNT

Waxahachie Smith series

NO FINGER ON THE TRIGGER
SLIP GUN
(   )
CURE THE TEXAS FEVER

Alvin Dustine "Cap" Fog series

ALVIN FOG, TEXAS RANGER
RAPIDO CLINT
THE JUSTICE OF COMPANY "Z"
(   )
CAP FOG, TEXAS RANGER, MEET
  MR. J. G. REEDER

THE RETURN OF RAPIDO CLINT
  AND MR. J. G. REEDER
RAPIDO CLINT STRIKES BACK

The Rockabye County series

THE SIXTEEN DOLLAR SHOOTER
THE LAWMEN OF ROCKABYE
  COUNTY
THE SHERIFF OF ROCKABYE
  COUNTY
THE PROFESSIONAL KILLERS
THE 1/4 SECOND DRAW
THE DEPUTIES
POINT OF CONTACT
THE OWLHOOT
RUN FOR THE BORDER
BAD HOMBRE
TEXAS TEAMWORK

Bunduki series

BUNDUKI
BUNDUKI AND DAWN
SACRIFICE FOR THE QUAGGA
  GOD
FEARLESS MASTER OF THE
  JUNGLE

Miscellaneous titles

J. T.'S HUNDREDTH
J. T.'S LADIES
MORE J. T.'S LADIES
J. T.'S LADIES RIDE AGAIN
IS-A-MAN
WANTED! BELLE STARR
SLAUGHTER'S WAY
TWO MILES TO THE BORDER
BLONDE GENIUS
(Written in collaboration with Peter
  Clawson)

*   *Denotes title awaiting publication.*
(   )   *Denotes position in which a proposed title will be*
placed.

Author's Note

When supplying us with the information from which we produce our books, one of the strictest rules imposed upon us by the present-day members of what we call the "Hardin, Fog, and Blaze" clan and the "Counter" family is that we *never* under *any* circumstances disclose their true identities, or their present whereabouts. Furthermore, we are instructed to *always* include enough inconsistencies where characters and locations are concerned to ensure that neither can happen inadvertently.

We would like to point out that the names of people who appear in this volume are those supplied to us by our informants in Texas and any resemblance with those of other persons, living or dead, is purely *coincidental*.

To save our "old hands" repetition, but for the benefit of new readers, we have included a "potted biography" of Mark Counter in the form of an Appendix.

We realize that, in our present permissive society, we could use the actual profanities employed by various people in the narrative. However, we do not concede that a spurious desire to create realism is any excuse to do so.

We refuse to pander to the current trendy usage of the metric system. Therefore, except when referring to the caliber of specific firearms traditionally measured in millimeters—i.e., Walther P-38, 9mm—we will continue to employ miles, yards, feet, inches, pounds, and ounces when quoting distances and weights.

Lastly, and of the *greatest* importance, we must stress that the attitudes and speech of the characters are put down as would have been the case at the period of this narrative and not as they would have it expressed.

J. T. EDSON
MELTON MOWBRAY
Leics.,
England

CURE THE
TEXAS
FEVER

J. T. Edson

A DELL BOOK

*For Ernie & Maggie Pope, mine host and
hostess at the Half Moon, Melton Mowbray.
Plus Sonia, Jane and Jean, who have
made me lose sixty-three pounds' weight by
restricting me to three Barbicans per lunch.*

Published by
Dell Publishing
a division of
Bantam Doubleday Dell Publishing Group, Inc.
1540 Broadway
New York, New York 10036

ISBN: 0-440-22215-X

Printed in the United States of America

Published simultaneously in Canada

June 1996

10 9 8 7 6 5 4 3 2 1
RAD

1

I'M NOT GOING TO FEEL HAPPY
ABOUT THE ANSWER

"Excuse me, sir," Edmund Dell said, entering the large
and elegantly furnished room on the first floor of a colo-
nial-style mansion not far from the Capitol Building in
Austin, Texas. He had an obsequious attitude that
seemed to augment his narrow features, mouse-brown
hair allowed to grow longer than was regarded as acceptable by some members of the community, and
overly neat attire in the latest Eastern fashion. Of me-
dium height, thin and pallid, he spoke with a nasal,
high-pitched, and somewhat whining Midwest accent.
"A *Mr.* and Mrs. Fog are here asking to see you."

"Very well," replied Matthew Anderson, owner of the
property and currently the governor of Texas. His voice
and appearance indicated that he had been born of affluent circumstances, was well educated, and had been
raised in the Lone Star State. Suspecting the man he
had found it politically advisable to accept as his private

secretary, he was aware of the honorific generally applied when announcing the male caller, and despite the way in which the message was delivered, he went on coldly, "Show *Captain* and Mrs. Fog in."

Watching Dell withdraw, closing the double doors even though the visitors were in view at the other side of the entrance hall, the governor frowned. After a few seconds, the doors were pushed open by the secretary and his visitors entered.

"Good afternoon, Freddie, Dusty. I trust you had a pleasant journey from the OD Connected?" Anderson greeted, rising and striding swiftly across the room with his right hand extended. Six feet tall, he had prematurely white hair and was sufficiently handsome to look well when attending any kind of function, whether it was leading a major parade on the anniversary of the Battle of San Jacinto[1] or gracing a private party regardless of the quality of the guests. He had an erect carriage, and despite the formal attire he had on, it was obvious he still possessed the firmly fleshed body of an outdoorsman. However, without waiting for a reply to his question, he went on, "That will be all, Dell. I'll ring if I should need you for anything."

"Yes, *sir,*" the secretary responded, looking just a trifle put out by the curt dismissal. However, instead of leaving immediately, he went on, "Er—after I've dealt with some correspondence, I have to go out for a short while, sir."

"That'll be all right," Anderson assented, having noticed the newcomers exchange glances during the brief interplay between himself and Dell. "If there's nothing else for you to do, you might as well call it a day and go home when you've finished whatever it is that's taking you away."

Turning, trying to convey an impression of injured dignity, Dell stalked rather than merely walked through the double doors, and shut them with as close to a bang as he dared. Then he went with greater haste than was his usual gait to the next room. Regardless of the way in which he had introduced the visitors, he was fully aware of their identity and status. Furthermore, he was sure he could guess why they had come to see the governor. If he was correct, he believed he might learn something of great use about a very important issue.

On being elected, wanting to disprove assertions made by the *Austin Intelligencer*—a newspaper owned and run by the liberal-radical faction in the capital—that his official appointments would be people to whom he and his campaign staff owed favors under the so-called spoils system, Anderson had yielded to their demands for "impartiality" by allowing Dell to remain in the capacity of governor's confidential secretary, a position he had held during the previous administration's period in office.

Although having incurred the dislike of his immediate superior, which probably would have happened even if the appointment had been made without duress, Dell had always been careful to avoid any glaring fault in the way he carried out his duties. On the other hand, he had continually been on the alert for any items that might be used to the detriment of his sponsors' political opponents.

At first, the task had not been arduous. Nor, as Dell had learned only minor items that would serve his sponsors' purposes, had it threatened to produce any chance of his duplicity being detected. However, the most recent instructions to procure information he had received were the most specific so far. Unfortunately for him, he was too deeply involved as a result of his earlier betrayals of confidence—and even less savory activities outside office hours—to be able to refuse the men who had arranged for his appointment.

Entering the room that served as his office, realizing he might be engaged for some time and having no de-

sire to be caught in the activity he was intending, since
he would be unable to furnish an acceptable reason for
doing so, the secretary turned the key in the lock. With
the precaution against anybody entering and discovering
what he was doing taken, instead of dealing with correspondence—not that he had had any intention of doing
this—he took a glass from the table on his desk. Crossing to the dividing wall, he placed the top of the glass on
it and rested his ear against the other end. As on the
other occasions he had eavesdropped in the same fashion, he found that he was able to overhear the conversation from which he had been prevented by his dismissal.

Listening, Dell soon concluded that he was finally acquiring far more important information on the subject
than had so far come his way.

Despite being a political appointee, the governor was
neither pompous nor so fond of hearing his own voice
that he had given the dismissal merely to impress his
influential visitors with his desire to speak to them
about a most important, urgent, and confidential issue.
Nothing in his demeanor indicated that he was aware
that, regardless of the high office he was currently holding, the two new arrivals in his study were held in
greater regard than he himself was by many people
throughout the Lone Star State. Always a realist and
having no jealousy in his character, he shared the sentiment. That was why he had called upon them: He felt
sure they would prove the best source of assistance he
could obtain to deal with the grave matter that had been
demanding the majority of his official attention for
some time.

Regardless of society and business still being regarded as basically a "man's world," it would not have
been difficult for any perceptive stranger who was privy
to the meeting to have understood why the taller of the
visitors was being treated with so much deference by the
governor. His attitude clearly went beyond his upbring-

ing as a Southern gentleman taught from early childhood to display politeness and respect for members of the so-called weaker sex. Nor would many people have considered her in such a light.

Five feet eight in height, Winifred Amelia "Miz Freddie" Fog had the impressive bearing that came naturally to a member of the British aristocracy and was an exceptionally fine figure of a woman. Her regally beautiful face had the rich golden tan of one in good health and was unlined by the passage of time. Beneath the stylish gray *toque*, her waved hair—with a center part, a short fringe, and the sides taken back into the "Cadogan" style that had become popular—was still coal black. She had on a close-fitting fashionable lightweight gray two-piece costume. Such were the magnificent Junoesque curves her close-to-hourglass figure still retained, she contrived to make the decorous attire seem as revealing as the most daring evening gown. Nevertheless, her expression and demeanor implied that she was a person with whom it would be ill-advised to trifle or take any other kind of liberty.

At first glance, the man by Freddie's side was far from an imposing sight. As Anderson had noticed on other occasions, unless there was danger or urgency in the situation, Captain Dustine Edward Marsden "Dusty" Fog tended to be overshadowed by his wife and most of the people around him. In fact, when first making his acquaintance in pacific circumstances, many strangers found it difficult to reconcile his physical appearance with the legendary reputation he had acquired during and since the War Between the States.[2]

Even aided by the high heels of his sharp-toed tan-colored cowhand-style boots, the male visitor was no more than five feet six in height. He had surrendered his black J. B. Stetson hat to the butler on arrival, revealing that he had neatly trimmed dusty-blond hair marked by a trace of graying at the temples. While he was moder-

ately good-looking in the white shirt with detachable
stiff collar and black necktie that were not regular items
of his attire, there was nothing particularly eye-catching
about his tanned and clean-shaven face. His two-piece
brown suit was well tailored to his fit, but he gave the
obviously expensive garments an appearance of being
somebody else's castoffs and they tended to emphasize
rather than detract from his small stature. Nor, despite
the rig having been produced by a master craftsman,
was he made more impressive-looking by wearing a
well-designed brown gunbelt—with twin bone-handled
Colt Civilian Model Peacemakers butt forward for a
cross-draw in its contoured holsters—about his waist.
Nevertheless, if one took the trouble to study him more
closely, there was a strength of will and intelligence beyond the norm about his features, and his muscular development was that of a Hercules in miniature.

"Why the armament, Dusty?" the governor inquired
after the formalities of arrival had been concluded and
his visitors were seated facing him across his large and
well-polished desk. "Are you expecting trouble?"

"Not especially," the small Texan replied. "But I
learned a long time back that the best way to stop trouble happening is to let folks know you're ready and able
to do just that."

"Should we be *expecting* trouble, Matt?" Freddie
asked. All the years she had spent in America had not
caused her to lose her upper-class British accent.

"Not that I know of," Anderson admitted, and a smile
came to his face. "Of course, Austin is civilized, but I
wouldn't know what's happening in wild and woolly
places like Rio Hondo County."

"I don't know about wild and woolly," Dusty drawled.
"Things're so quiet down to home that the Kid allows
he'll plumb die of boredom."

"You know why I asked if you would come and see
me?" the governor inquired, becoming serious. Al-

though he paused briefly, he continued before any reply could be given. "We have to find a cure for what newspapers up North are calling the 'Texas fever.'"

"We had a notion it might be something like that, Matt," Dusty said quietly. Like the man he was addressing, his voice had the accent of a well-educated Texan. As had often happened when they had met in the past, the governor forgot his size in mere feet and inches. By the sheer strength of his will in a crisis—and the subject under discussion ranked as that—he gave an impression of being the biggest person present. "And there's something we can do about it. We met up with a right smart young feller while we were on vacation last month. He's already done a fair amount of work trying to find out what causes the Texas fever and how to cure it. If we can bring him down to Texas, give him all the money and help he'll need, I reckon he's got a better-than-fair chance of coming up with the answers."

"If you should have any trouble getting the money out of those tightfisted gentlemen in the legislature," Freddie went on before Anderson could pose the question that had come to mind, "along with Colonel Goodnight and quite a few more of our big ranch-owning friends, Dawn and Mark Counter say they'll be willing to open their wallets and help out, and it goes without saying you can count on the Hardin, Fog, and Blaze clan to do the same—for a price, of course."

"There's *always* a price," Anderson declared, but with a smile. He felt sure neither a financial outlay nor any other costly personal favor at the expense of the state's taxpayers was required. However, he did not inquire further into that subject. Instead, he turned his gaze to his male visitor. "But you said *if* you can bring him down, Dusty."

"You know as well as I do that not everybody outside the state and even down here wants to see us with a sound and moneymaking cattle business," the small

Texan pointed out grimly. "And some of those who don't are mean enough—and have enough money behind them—to try to prevent it continuing to bring cash into Texas the way it does."

"That's true," the governor admitted. "But surely he'll be safe enough at either the OD Connected or Mark Counter's MC?"

"We could likely keep him safe at either place," the big Texan conceded. "But it won't help him settle down to his work if we have to keep fighting off jaspers figuring to make wolf bait of him so's he can't finish it."

"You think it could come to that?"

"I'm certain *sure* it could come to that!"

"And you've got something in mind that could let him carry out his work without any such interruption?" Anderson said, the words more a statement than a question.

"Why, sure," Dusty drawled in a matter-of-fact tone. "We'll have him sneaked down to Texas and, if we're lucky and his whereabouts stay secret, he won't be found before he's through."

"Secrets have a nasty way of getting leaked out," Anderson warned, despite feeling sure that the possibility had already been taken into account.

"And that's the truthful true," the small Texan agreed.

"But, of course, we don't have to worry about *that* happening over what we're discussing here," the beautiful woman asserted in a definite fashion, which brought a mocking sneer to the face of the man listening in the next room.

"That's for sure," Dusty supported, and the air of smug satisfaction being displayed by Dell increased. "Anyways, to make sure nothing goes wrong, we're going to have a real good man going to fetch him and ride herd on him until he finishes the chore."

"Would that be you, Mark, or the Ysabel Kid?" the

governor queried, thinking that any one of the three would be well able to cope with the task.[3]

"None of us," the small Texan replied.

"Why not?" Anderson asked, showing surprise.

"No matter which of us it was," Dusty explained, "he'd be sure to get noticed and talked about no matter where he went."

"Then just *who* do you have in mind?" the governor wanted to know, and seeing the glances exchanged by his visitors, continued in a tone redolent of one who was resigned to an unpleasant fate. "Something tells me I'm not going to feel happy about the answer."

"I don't see why," Dusty drawled, and although he rubbed his forefingers together, he went on without giving the name of the candidate. "Like I said, he's a real good man and, backed by the reward you can offer him, he'll do everything he can to see Frank *Smith* gets the work done."

"Reward?" Anderson queried, despite having noticed the emphasis placed on the surname "Smith" and guessing the answer. Glancing involuntarily at his hands, the forefingers extended, he continued, "Then that's the price you meant, Freddie, and it is *him?"*

"That's our price, Matt, and it is *him,"* the beautiful woman confirmed with a smile. "A pardon will give him what he's wanted for years: to be able to live peacefully in Texas without having some bounty hunter or overofficious lawman come after him. He's kindhearted and doesn't want to make life rough for them."

"Do you think he'll take a chance on coming back *before* the pardon's been granted?" the governor asked.

"I *know* he will," Dusty asserted with conviction. "Fact being, we've already been in touch with him by telegraph. He said, 'Why, sure,' and he'll be coming back to Texas in a couple of weeks' time."

"And you'll be meeting him ready to help out should

any lawman remember he's still wanted?" Anderson guessed.

"Not *me,*" Dusty corrected. "We figure that's what would be expected and conclude to play sneaky. So it'll be Mark on hand to say 'Howdy, you-all.' He'll be better placed to do it, seeing's how they'll be meeting up where you might figure those white-faced cattle that some of us are counting on to replace the longhorns come from."

"Does he know what's wanted from him?" the governor inquired, without asking for more specific information regarding the location at which the rendezvous was to take place.

"Not all of it," the small Texan admitted. "But Mark'll tell him everything when they meet up."

"In that case," Anderson said with a ring of assurance in his voice, "Mark can tell him from *me* that he'll be given his pardon if he can keep Mr. Smith safe and well for long enough to find the cure for the Texas fever. When that's been done, he'll have more than earned it."

There was an expression of satisfaction mingled with disappointment on Dell's face as he removed the mouth of the glass from the wall and crossed to replace it on his desk. Although he had been correct in his assumption that the subject of the meeting would be of great interest to the man to whom he was under orders to report such things, he realized that at least one important piece of information was missing. Nevertheless, he felt he had taken enough risks and, as the talking next door had turned to general matters such as a reception the governor was holding later in the day and to which the visitors were invited, he drew some satisfaction from knowing that he had overheard everything of consequence that was going to be said on the matter.

Unlocking and opening the door, the secretary glanced in each direction along the entrance hall. Nobody was in sight, and the same proved to be the case when he stepped onto the wide porch. The four-passenger surrey in which the Fogs had arrived was still standing at the hitching rail with the saddled horse ridden by the young man, dressed after the fashion of a cowhand, who had accompanied them to the mansion. The latter was nowhere to be seen, but this did not surprise Dell. Although no instructions had been given, knowing the butler invariably dealt with such matters without requiring any, the secretary concluded that the cowhand had been taken to the kitchen to be given a meal or some kind of liquid refreshment.

Putting the absence of the third visitor from his mind and satisfied that he had collected the information without detection, Dell went across the porch so he could deliver it without delay. The governor always kept a horse and buggy available for use, and Dell would have summoned a servant to fetch it for him in normal circumstances. In fact, wishing to establish his superior status around the mansion, he invariably did even when going to the nearby Capitol Building or the boardinghouse where he lived. However, although his destination was farther away than either and in a part of town he did not usually frequent, he had no desire for it to become known to the driver. Therefore, he considered it advisable to go there on foot.

1. *Taking place on Thursday, April 21, 1836, the Battle of San Jacinto was the culmination of the struggle by the people of Texas to free them-selves from Mexican rule. Information about some of the events leading up to the battle is given in the Ole Devil Hardin series.*
2. *Information about the career and family background of Captain Dustine Edward Marsden "Dusty" Fog can be found in most volumes of the Civil War and Floating Outift series.*
2a. *The first meeting between Dusty Fog and his wife when she was Lady Winifred Phoebe Besgrove-Woodstole, why she was living in Mulrooney, Kansas, under the alias "Freddie Wood," and the events leading up to their marriage are told in* THE MAKING OF A LAWMAN, THE TROUBLE BUSTERS, *and* DECISION FOR DUSTY FOG.
2b. *"Freddie Woods" also appears in* CARDS AND COLTS; THE

CODE OF DUSTY FOG; THE GENTLE GIANT; THE FORTUNE HUNTERS; Part Six, "The Butcher's Fiery End," J. T.'S LADIES; *and* THE WHIP AND THE WAR LANCE.

2c. *"Miz Freddie" Fog makes a guest appearance under her married name in* NO FINGER ON THE TRIGGER.

3. *Information about the career, family background, and special qualifications of the Ysabel Kid can be found in various volumes of the Civil War and Floating Outfit series.*

2

DUSTY FOG'S STILL A MAN TO STAND ASIDE FROM

"And that was how they left it," Edmund Dell concluded, directing the words at the curtain hanging over the hatch in the wall of the room he had entered on his arrival at a small saloon on the fringes of "respectable" Austin. His voice held the self-satisfied timbre of one convinced he had achieved something beyond the abilities of another. "So I thought I had better come to tell you straightaway."

"You didn't hear *anything* else?" demanded a masculine voice from the next room. It had an accent that was impossible to define yet was suggestive of one with a good education. There was also an underlying cruelty and menace that the secretary found disturbing. "Not even the name of this feller they're sending for, or where Mark Counter'll be meeting up with him?"

"N-no—!" Dell gulped, startled by the malignancy

with which the questions were uttered and losing his smug expression.

"Then all the trouble those softshell friends of yours went to so's you'd be inside the Capitol Building and close to the governor still hasn't been worth much," growled the invariably unseen speaker to whom the secretary was under orders to deliver the news whenever he learned anything concerning the subject about which he had just finished speaking. "Has it?"

Although the secretary did not intend to state his point of view in so many words, he thought his efforts of the day were being belittled without cause. Until that afternoon, when reporting to the man in the same fashion, he had had nothing more to tell than that there was a regular delivery of newspapers from all over the state and elsewhere containing articles about the situation regarding the so-called Texas fever and how the governor read each one with great care.

Even without having come to know Matthew Anderson as well as a more competent spy would have done, Dell had concluded he was very concerned over the threat that was posed to the economy of Texas by the mysterious disease and was determined to take whatever steps might prove necessary to combat it. His reaction to the coming of Captain and Mrs. Fog, about whom the secretary had heard much in spite of the way in which the announcement of their arrival was made—especially regarding their connection with the cattle business—had suggested that he was calling upon them for assistance, and the subsequent conversation had verified this was the case.

"I've told you that Anderson is taking steps to have a cure found for the Texas fever," the secretary pointed out sullenly.

"And I already *knew* he would be," the unseen man growled. "That's why *you* were told to find out what those steps were going to be."

"I've let you know that he's called in Fog to help him," Dell objected with closer to a whining petulance than defiance. "And how they're going to have somebody fetch this Frank Smith, whoever he might be, and have somebody guarding him while he's looking for the cure."

"I never thought for even a goddamned minute they'd let him do his work without having him well guarded while he's at it," the man in the next room stated sarcastically. "So it'd be a big help if we knew who the feller doing the guarding's going to be, or where he'll be collecting and taking Smith."

"From what I heard," Dell said, "they *won't* be going to either Fog's OD Connected or Mark Counter's MC."

"That sure narrows it down," the unseen speaker commented, but without showing any hint of being impressed and mollified by the latest piece of information. "There's only the rest of Texas for to go hunting around, which can't be more than a few thousand square miles. Knowing who the feller they're going to use as Smith's guide is could help us find him."

"They never mentioned his name, or where he could be meeting and going to take Smith," the secretary reminded sulkily, wondering what would happen if he should lunge forward and jerk aside the curtain. Despite realizing that recognizing the man beyond it might put him in a stronger position where their future negotiations were concerned, in view of the coldly menacing manner in which he was always addressed, he lacked the courage to make the attempt. "Only that he's been sent for and Counter's going to meet him when he reaches Texas in a couple of weeks—and that will be happening at Brownsville."

"How'd you figure that out?" the unseen speaker inquired, his voice still giving no suggestion of an improvement in attitude.

"From what I've heard, that's where most of those

white-faced cattle Fog mentioned arrive from Europe,"
the secretary explained. "He said that was where the
meeting would be, and as Anderson didn't ask any more
questions, I realized he must mean Brownsville, because
that's where most of them are being landed after they've
been shipped over from England."

"Wasn't *anything* else said?"

"Well, yes. There was something, but it wasn't anything useful."

"*I'll* be the judge of that!"

"Whoever they're sending for is wanted for a crime,"
Dell explained, forgetting the mention Dusty Fog had
made about Mark Counter being better situated than
himself to carry out the rendezvous.

"How do you know?" the man asked, unaware that a
vital piece of information had not been supplied.

"The Fog woman said whoever it is would want a
pardon for helping," Dell answered, wishing he could
see how the news was being received. "But knowing that
doesn't help any unless I can find out his name, and I've
a feeling doing it won't be easy. In fact, I've already
learned all I can without running the risk of being
caught at it."

"Then take whatever goddamned risks you have to!"
commanded the man in the next room. "I want to know
who the feller is."

"My *friends* wouldn't want me to get caught doing it!"
Dell protested in alarm. "I'd be fired, and they need me
there!"

"And I need to know his name," the unseen man
pointed out savagely, concluding that the secretary's
concern was caused by the possibility of forfeiting a lu-
crative position rather than worrying over the reaction
of his "friends" to its loss. "There're fathers in Fort
Worth who didn't like the kind of games you and your
two softshell schoolteacher buddies used to play with
their little boys after class. You got clean away when the

other two stretched hemp for it. But unless you get me *everything* I want to know, the folks in Cowtown are going to find out where you're at. I'm getting paid good money to make sure *nobody* finds the cure for the Texas fever, and I'm not going to let your getting fired spoil my chances of doing it. So you'd best get me what I want to know, and *fast*, or I'll let them folks up there know where you can be found."

"B-but—!" Dell began, and his demeanor showed something closer to fear than just alarm over the threat.

"You'd better get going," the man in the next room interrupted. "And don't be long before you come back with the feller's name and everything else you can get on him. I'm not known for being strong on patience."

Opening his mouth to make a protest against the ultimatum, Dell thought better of it. He suspected that, although he could not see beyond the curtain covering the hatch through which the conversation was taking place, his interrogator was able to watch him. With that disturbing possibility in mind, he tried to keep hidden his animosity and the alarm that had been aroused by the threat. Swinging around with what little dignity he could muster, he went quickly to the door that he had locked on entering. Turning the key, he drew it open and was about to go out when he found he was unable to do so.

"Is this whereat the game is?" inquired a voice with a Texas drawl and the somewhat slurred timbre suggestive of intoxication.

Standing just outside the room, holding a wad of paper money in his left hand, the speaker was in his early twenties. He had a bronzed, freckled, pugnaciously good-looking face. A flat cap of Eastern style sat at an angle on a mop of untidy fiery red hair and he was dressed in a three-piece brown suit, a white shirt with a detachable celluloid collar, and a multihued necktie. However, instead of being some form of town dweller's footwear, his black boots had the calf-high legs, sharp toes, and high heels that experience had taught cowhands were best suited to the specialized needs of their work. Despite this indication of him being one of that hard-riding, hardworking and harder-playing breed, dressed up fancy for a visit to the city, he did not appear to be armed in any way.

"What game?" Dell snapped.

Even while speaking, the secretary wondered why the man confronting him seemed vaguely familiar. Having no regard for cowhands regardless of how they might be dressed, because they never treated him with the kind of servile respect his middle class–middle management parents had always encouraged him to believe was his rightful due, he did not number any of them among his circle of acquaintances. Despite something almost forgotten stirring in his memory, he could not bring it back to full recollection in his disturbed frame of mind.

"I heard tell there's a poker game for decent stakes down here," the red-haired Texan declared, retaining his position. "Which being, having only run across pikers wanting to play for nickels and dimes since I hit town and, being flush with payoff money, I concluded I'd drift on by 'n' sit in for a spell."

Before Dell could repeat the denial or force the nagging thought to take further shape, the young man stepped forward. Startled into an involuntary retreat by the sudden and unexpected movement, Dell was followed across the threshold. His gaze flickered to the curtain and he was relieved to see it was still in position across the hatch.

"Dagnab it!" the Texan growled, gazing around the otherwise unoccupied room. "Maybe it's next door."

Thrusting the money into his jacket's inside right pocket while speaking, the redhead strolled over with deceptive speed and, standing to one side, jerked open the curtain. However, his curiosity was not satisfied. In the interim, whoever was on the other side had closed and, as proved by the push the Texan gave it, fastened the wooden hatch. Giving a casual-seeming shrug, he walked with a similar appearance of nonchalance past Dell. Following him, the secretary watched with some alarm as he tried the next door and found that it was locked. Although he did not receive any response from inside when he knocked, six men gathered around a nearby table tensed a little as if expecting something to happen.

Five of the group, four white men and a Mexican, looked like typical range-country drifters who—although not of the top quality—made their living by selling their guns. Taller than the others and of Caucasian birth, the sixth was equally tough-looking. However, his features were reddened rather than having been tanned by long exposure to the elements, and he did not have the appearance of one who spent much time outdoors. A brown jacket of Eastern cut and a tan Stetson in the style of Texas were hanging on the back of his chair. He wore a white shirt, black string tie, brown trousers, and Hersome gaiter boots. Where the rest carried their weapons on gunbelts, his Colt Artillery Model Peacemaker revolver was in an open-fronted spring-retention shoulder holster suspended under his left armpit.

"Aw, hell!" The redhead sighed after having knocked again without receiving any sign that the room was occupied. Swinging on his heel with an expression suggesting annoyance, he directed his gaze to the six men and, giving no indication of noticing the coldly threatening way they were studying him, he continued, "Looks like I heard wrong. Do you fellers know where I can find me some action?"

"Try the Iron Mistress down to Bowie," suggested the tallest of the group, referring to a saloon in the poorer section of the town. Despite his attire, his accent indicated he was from northern Texas. "What I've heard, you'll 'most always find a game or two going on there."

"Gracias," the redhead thanked, and he started to turn away. "I reckon that's just what I'll do."

Having gone by the young Texan while the request for information was being made to the group at the table, Dell almost scuttled across the barroom. He was just about to pass through the batwing doors when, causing him to pause momentarily and look over his shoulder, memory flooded back to bring further alarm and consternation in its wake. He remembered having watched through the window by the front door of the mansion as the Fogs were approaching along the drive from the main gate. The woman was driving the four-passenger surrey, and they were accompanied by a cowhand who was not brought with them to meet the governor. The secretary had not been interested in the young man at the time. On setting out for the saloon, seeing that the young man's horse was hitched by the surrey, Dell had decided that he was still on the premises and forgot about him.

Now the situation had changed drastically.

Except for the way in which they were dressed, the rider at the mansion and the apparently not-quite-sober young man here at the saloon were so alike that they must be brothers and most probably twins!

Although Dell realized that there could be some completely innocuous explanation for the redhead's presence, drinking and gambling forming a notable part of cowhand behavior when they were in town, his every instinct warned that such was not the case on this occasion. It seemed highly unlikely that coincidence alone was responsible for the brother of the rider with the Fogs to not only have selected the saloon to which the secretary had come, but to believe there was a poker game in one of the two rooms where he had been talking with the unseen man.

With a chilling sense of apprehension, Dell concluded that there was only one explanation for the unexpected turn of affairs: His treachery had been suspected. Therefore, he had been followed by one of Dusty Fog's hired hands—whom he would be less likely to notice than anybody the governor could assign to the task—to obtain evidence of his perfidy.

A sensation of terror flooded through the secretary as he arrived at the unpalatable conclusion. On his return to the mansion and the arrival of the young Texan to tell where he had been, he would be questioned about his reason for paying the visit, and he was unable to think of any reply that would offer a believable explanation. Therefore, having provided what could be considered as proof that he was betraying his trust, the very least he could expect was to be discharged from the well-paid position that his sponsors had taken considerable trouble to obtain for him.

However, being completely self-centered, Dell was less concerned with the likelihood of losing his post than the possible reaction of the man with whom he had been talking if he was no longer able to offer the chance of acquiring further information. While they had never met face-to-face as far as the secretary was aware, it was obvious the other had obtained knowledge of a very unsavory incident in his past that he had believed was well concealed. What was more, he felt certain that the threat to expose his misdeeds in Fort Worth would be carried out.

Then another, even more chilling thought struck Dell. Should the man in the other room learn the identity of the young Texan and suspect the truth, he would not hesitate before taking steps to ensure that Dell could not tell the governor about the reason for their clandestine meetings.

Having arrived at the last and most frightening conclusion by the time he reached the street, the secretary decided that flight was the only answer to his deadly predicament. However, he realized that he must return to Governor Anderson's mansion before he could commence his escape. Because he did not trust the owner of the room he rented in town—an elderly widow with a penchant for going through her lodgers' personal property in their absence—there were certain items locked in his desk that he had no desire to leave behind. In fact, some of them were of a nature that would serve as an inducement for his sponsors to supply financial assistance to help him get away even if they could not intercede on his behalf with the man to whom he had been ordered to report.

If Dell had looked into the barroom before taking his departure, he might have become even more alarmed. Instead, being aware that the redhead was strolling toward the batwing doors, he hurried off in the direction from which he had come without a backward glance.

As soon as the red-haired Texan left the saloon, the door at which he had knocked opened a trifle. However, even if he had glanced to his rear, he would not have learned anything about the identity of the occupant. The man with whom Dell had spoken remained inside and made sure he could not be seen by anyone in the barroom. Acting in response to a softly spoken command of "Pampa, get in here!" the tallest of the six hard cases—whose name came from the town seat of Gray County in northern Texas, where he claimed to have his origins—rose and went swiftly in obedience to the summons.

"Do any of you know who that red-topped young jasper was?" Pampa asked on rejoining his companions after being absent for about a minute.

"Sure," replied the shortest of the Americans wearing range clothes, looking surprised. "He's one of the Blaze twins who ride for Dusty Fog down to the OD Connected in Rio Hondo County, but I couldn't say which of 'em he might be."

"The hell you say!" Pampa growled. After striding to a window on the front of the building and conducting an examination of the street, he went back into the room at the rear instead of rejoining his companions. On emerging, he crossed to the table and said, "I've got a chore to handle and so have you. The boss and me figure that lavender boy he's had spying on the governor'll be running scared, happen he reckons he's been followed here, which I reckon he did, the way he acted just afore he left. That being, he'd be right easy to be made to talk. So I'm going to make sure he can't. For all he made out he'd come here looking for a card game and was going down to the Iron Mistress, the Blaze kid's watching the front from an alley across the street. Happen he comes after me, you've got to stop him should he come nosing around in here again, or goes 'round the back."

"The hell you say!" barked the shortest of the men, showing an alarm that at least two of the others duplicated. "I told you who he is."

"You told me," Pampa admitted, putting on his hat and looking disdainful. "So what difference does that make?"

"There wasn't nothing said about us going up against that OD Connected bunch when you took us on," the supplier of the information reminded sullenly.

"You've been hired to go up against anybody's I tell you to," Pampa declared.

"We're not locking horns with *that* crowd," the shortest man asserted, and the rest of the group mumbled concurrence. "You don't hear so much about him these days as you used to a few years back, but, by all accounts, Dusty Fog's still a man to stand aside from when he gets riled, and there's others in the crew, 'specially the Ysabel Kid, who's even worse."

"And there's *nothing's* is more like' to get them riled

than for us to make wolf bait of one of Dusty Fog's kin,"
supported the second tallest of the hard cases, having
nodded vehemently when the second name was mentioned. "Which we're not getting paid anywheres near
enough for us to do something that stupid."

"And I didn't say nothing about you making wolf bait
of him," Pampa pointed out coldly. "Fact being, the
boss said for me to tell you he didn't want no killing. All
you have to do is stop him nosing around here, following me, or going 'round the back afore the boss's got
clear. Should any of 'em come off, make it look like he
got caught up by accident in a private fistfight, or was
attacked and rolled for his pay, which looked to be a fair
sum when he was waving it around in here, should he go
'round the back. There's five of you to just the one of
him, so you should be able to do *that.*"

3

GET THE HELL OUT OF IT,
JOHN!

Arising out of the belief that he was far too intelligent
and shrewd for his treachery while acting as Governor
Anderson's secretary to be suspected, Edmund Dell had
been amused to hear Mrs. Freddie Fog claim that there
was no chance of the conversation taking place in the
office at the mansion becoming known to anybody other
than herself, her husband, and their host. Therefore, he
had fallen into a trap that she had laid.

As was the case with Dusty Fog, despite frequent suggestions that they should do so, Freddie had always declined to take any active part in the political life of
Texas. Nevertheless, they contrived to keep in touch
with many things that were taking place in and around
the state capital. It had not gone unnoticed by them
that, while none were of a serious nature, certain confidential matters detrimental to supporters of the governor had been brought to public notice since he took

office. Having faith in the integrity of Matthew Anderson, they had still concluded that this leakage of information stemmed from somebody in his entourage. Learning of the pressure that caused him to retain Dell as his secretary, they had believed they would find the latter was responsible.

On receiving a letter sent by the governor's wife—which they learned later was dispatched without Dell's knowledge—asking them ostensibly to attend a reception at the State Capitol Building, and being aware of how gravely Anderson regarded the matter of the so-called Texas fever, Freddie and Dusty had concluded that he wished to discuss it with them without this becoming known to anybody else. Having already started in motion a scheme of their own to try to find a solution to the problem, the Fogs were pleased at being granted the opportunity to gain official support for one of its more delicate aspects from Anderson.

In addition to the main issue taking them there, before setting out for Austin, Freddie and Dusty had concocted a ruse that they hoped might lead to the exposure of the one responsible for betraying confidential subjects. With this in mind, they had brought three men from the OD Connected ranch who they believed would help bring about the unmasking of the traitor. In part, the assignments were a reward for the hard work recently performed around the spread by their identical twin nephews, Charles "Charlie" and Henry "Hank" Blaze. The third member of the group was chosen because it was deemed that he might be even less noticeable than either of the brothers and, unless he came into contact with somebody who knew the true state of affairs, was unlikely to be associated with them during the work that might need to be carried out.

In accordance with the plan, only Hank accompanied his aunt and uncle all the way to the mansion. As it was his task to try to follow anybody who left on horseback or by some kind of vehicle after the meeting with the governor, he had come on horseback instead of sharing the four-passenger surrey. While Dell was correct in as-suming that the redhead had been invited indoors for refreshments by the butler, he had contrived to keep watch on the front of the building. Seeing the secretary depart on foot, he had decided that no action was re-quired on his part and remained at his point of vantage in case somebody else should leave.

Charlie had not been assigned the task of carrying out the following on foot if it should be needed, because he was the older brother by some fifteen minutes. Because he and his sibling shared the typical cowhand aversion to moving around except on the back of a horse, they had spun a coin to decide who took the duty. In accor-dance with Freddie's instructions, to lessen the chance of his resemblance to Hank being observed by whoever he found himself following, he had changed into his "go to town" attire before leaving the hotel at which the rest of the party from the OD Connected were staying.

Either the precaution had paid off or, more likely, Dell had been too absorbed to notice that he was being followed. Nevertheless, Charlie concluded that the physical resemblance between himself and Hank did not go undetected when he confronted the secretary in the saloon. Nor had his attempt to discover with whom Dell had been speaking in the back room achieved any result other than to strengthen his supposition that news of the meeting between his relatives and the governor had been reported to whoever was beyond the hatch in the wall. Judging by the menacing attitude of the half-dozen hard cases seated near the second door that it would be extremely unwise to try to take the matter further at that time, he had sought to convey the impression of being nothing more than a slightly drunk young cow-hand in search of a game of poker. Much to his relief,

Dell had not said anything to clarify the matter and he was left unhindered to go on with his assignment.

Despite Charlie's having been instructed to follow anybody who left the mansion and find out where they were going, he had decided not to report back to his aunt and uncle immediately. Instead, showing the kind of initiative Freddie and Dusty had always encouraged, he concluded that he would be better employed by trying to discover whom Dell had come to visit at the saloon. His instincts suggested that the visit was connected with the meeting his aunt and uncle were having with the governor, and he felt sure they would be interested in knowing to whom the information was passed. Therefore, he had crossed the street and was keeping watch from an alley.

Seeing the tallest hard case leave the building and set off in a way suggesting that he did not wish to be detected by the secretary, the young Texan concluded that a change of plan was required. Letting out a grunt of annoyance, he stepped forward. Glancing in each direction along the almost deserted street, he crossed and made his way along the alley separating the saloon from its neighbor. A quick look around the end of the building failed to locate anybody in the immediate vicinity. However, as he started to walk forward with the intention of looking through the window of the room into which he had been unable to gain admittance, the rear door opened. Three of the other white hard cases and the Mexican emerged. As they walked forward in a loose arrowhead formation, the Mexican holding a cigarette in his left hand, advanced more quickly than his companions and patted his pockets with the right.

"Hey, *amigo*," the Mexican said, turning in Charlie's direction. "Do you have a match, *por favor?*"

"Why, sure," the redhead admitted amiably, and made as if to reach into his trousers' right pocket.

Satisfied that his intentions were not suspected, the

Mexican allowed the cigarette to slip from his fingers and lunged forward. Aware of what he was meaning to do, the three white hard cases also speeded up their advance. Far from being taken unawares, Charlie proved that he had anticipated something of the kind and responded to the threat with commendable speed. Changing its direction and knotting it into a fist, showing the kind of skill and precision that implied he was well trained in fistfighting, Charlie shot his right hand forward. Its rock-hard knuckles met the Mexican's nose with considerable force, snapping back his head and bringing blood from his nostrils as he reeled away from his intended victim. At the same time, his enormously roweled spurs became entangled and caused him to lose his balance. He went down onto his rump and, the impact of his arrival driving all the remaining breath from his lungs, remained seated in a bewildered condition.

Nor did the first of the white hard cases fare much better. Instead of relying on his fistic prowess this time, Charlie, bending at the waist so the hands reaching for him passed harmlessly above him, waited until the man ran up against him and tilted forward. Then, putting the strength of his wiry body into a surging heave, he straightened up to cause his would-be assailant to turn a half-somersault over his back. However, a blow from the second white man struck him on the side of the face and sent him staggering. Keeping his balance and coming to a halt, he blocked a blow from the third hard case and counterpunched with the kind of ability and power he had shown from the beginning. Even as his blow sent its recipient stumbling away, he remembered that there was another member of the party from the table to be accounted for.

The recollection came a moment too late.

Having remained just inside the saloon while his companions emerged, still feeling misgivings over the orders they had received from Pampa and wanting to disassociate himself should the others go too far in their attack upon the well-connected young Texan, the shortest member of the group was startled to see their efforts meeting so little success. However, concluding that he must take some kind of action unless he wished his refraining to be reported by his companions as being responsible for the failure of the attack, he felt he could turn things in their favor. Darting through the back door, he arrived quickly enough to smash his interlocked hands against the back of the redhead's neck before his presence could be detected.

Taken unawares by the violent assault from his rear, Charlie was driven forward. Going down to alight on hands and knees before he could regain his equilibrium, he realized that he was in a most serious predicament. Although neither the Mexican nor the first white attacker had returned to the fray, the latter was starting to get up. What was more, the other two hard cases were coming toward him, and he knew he could not assume a more suitable position for defense—or take a more positive means of protecting himself—quickly enough to allow him to fend off the forthcoming attack.

When the group had left the saloon, the street behind the building had been deserted except for their intended victim. However, as Charlie was being knocked down and his white assailants moved in to continue their attack, a figure came around the corner of a building at the other side. If the attackers had noticed him, they probably would have dismissed him as being of no importance.

Not much over five feet five, with a slim build, the new arrival was clad in a brown three-piece suit, white shirt, black necktie, and Hersome gaiter boots. In his right hand he was carrying what appeared to be a straight and stout walking stick made of well-polished bamboo. Despite his Occidental attire, his features were those of an Oriental—and one getting along in years.

His hair was not hanging down in a pigtail, but he could have been following the habit many Chinamen thought advisable to adopt because of the unwanted attentions a pigtail frequently attracted in the Western world, and tucked it under the black derby hat he was wearing.

On seeing what was happening, the small Oriental began to act in an unusual manner. Faced with such a situation, and having no desire to become involved in what most of the participants would consider a private matter, a Chinaman of that age—or even one much younger—would in almost every case either have gone back in the direction from which he had come or hurried past with eyes averted. Instead of taking either course, the newcomer gave a shout in his native tongue and advanced even more rapidly.

"Get the hell out of it, John!" snarled the attacker who had landed the first blow on Charlie, employing the form of address frequently given an unknown Chinaman.

When the order was ignored, the man let out a profanity and, leaving his companions to continue moving in on the redhead, turned his attention to the Oriental. Taking into account that height, weight, and age were all in his favor—and that he had never seen a Chinaman show any kind of aggressive tendencies—he did not believe he would have any difficulty in driving off the imprudent intruder, and he was enough of a bully to revel in the opportunity. However, he soon discovered that he was in error in that assumption.

Going into a lunge that a French Creole fencing master would have admired, the Oriental sent the metal tip of the sturdy bamboo stick digging into the hard case's solar plexus. Although he lacked the knowledge to appreciate the finer aspects of the attack, the white man could—and later did, to the accompaniment of much profanity—testify to its painful effectiveness. In spite of the deliverer's comparatively small stature, the jab was hard enough to cause its recipient to let out an agonized belch, stumble to the rear—his hands grabbing at the point of impact—and begin to fold over.

Paying no further attention to his would-be attacker, the little Oriental leaped onward with a speed that seemed out of keeping with one of his years. On coming into range, he continued to wield the stout cane in a most efficacious manner. In fact, whether grasping it by one hand or both, he employed it to deliver either jabs or blows. Nor, despite the rapidity with which he moved, did they arrive too lightly to be ignored.

Spluttering curses, the white men gave their attention to the rescuer. One managed to catch hold of the cane but was compelled to release it by being kicked in the stomach. At almost the same moment the small man, seeming to have eyes in the back of his head, so quickly did he respond, blocked a punch sent his way with his left arm and retaliated by driving its elbow hard into the would-be attacker's chest, causing an involuntary retreat of a few steps.

Being poked or struck as was most convenient to their assailant—whose dexterity implied long training in such a way of fighting—and either motion proving equally painful to the recipient, the rapidity of the small Oriental's attack scattered the hard cases from around Charlie. Under different circumstances, particularly when in contention against an assailant they believed to be Chinese, one or another of them would have drawn a gun and ended the attack by using it. However, they were all mindful of the young Texan's important family connections, and thinking these would extend to his rescuer, did not want to start shooting.

"Get the hell out of here!" yelled the last man to leave the saloon, seeing faces peering through a rear window of the building across the street and realizing there could be an intervention, or at least witnesses to help describe them when the redhead reported the attack to the town marshal.

Sharing the sentiment that prompted it, the other white men were only too willing to carry out the order, and they immediately joined the speaker in starting to hurry away. However, the same did not apply to the Mexican. Having regained his feet and stared for a few seconds at the blood from his nose that was smeared over both palms, he let out a profanity in his native tongue. Then, forgetting the warning that no weapons be used that had been given before they left the saloon, he reached across with his right hand and slid the long-bladed fighting knife from the sheath on his belt. Despite being wild with fury, the way in which he lunged toward the little Oriental indicated that he was dangerously skilled in the use of such a weapon.

Hearing the yell of "Behind you, Danny!" from Charlie, the small man whirled around. He took in what was happening with a quick glance, and his right fingers gave a twist and tug on the handle of the cane. It turned, and from inside the bamboo emerged a long, brightly shining, slightly curved steel blade with a "reversed Wharncliffe" point. Even as the other weapon was driving his way in the low and deadly ripping slash favored by competent knife fighters, he retaliated. Nor, being handled by one so competent in its use, did having a twenty-eight-inch blade make it clumsy.

Flashing around, the edge of the sword—it warranted no other designation—proved to be razor sharp. Biting into the Mexican's arm just above the wrist, it passed through the bone and sinews as if they offered no more resistance than a sheet of paper. A scream of agony burst from the Mexican as, with blood spurting from severed veins and arteries, his hand and the knife dropped to the ground. Once again he stumbled backward, but this time his injury was far more severe.

Already starting to join his companions in their hurried departure, the last hard case from the saloon saw what had happened to the Mexican. Being quicker-witted than his companions, as was proved by his allowing them to commence the attack upon Charlie while he remained in the background, he realized that such an injury would slow down the other's escape to an unacceptable extent. What was more, he appreciated how allowing the wounded man to fall into the hands of the law was most inadvisable. Although Pedro was unaware of their employer's identity, he could name all the rest of them and almost certainly would as revenge for being deserted. Feeling sure the local law would take action with alacrity in view of the important people who were involved, he knew this must not be allowed to happen.

With those considerations in mind, the hard case took what he considered to be the only way out. Bringing his Colt from its holster, he sent a bullet into the staggering Mexican's chest. However, he was not allowed to make certain that he had ended all chances of information being supplied by his victim.

Given the respite he had needed so badly, Charlie had been able to clear his head and come to his feet. He was just erect when the shot crashed out, and he responded immediately. Although there had been no sign of his having a weapon on his person, he had been disinclined to engage in the task to which he was assigned without being armed. As had often been the case with other things in the past, he found himself grateful that his uncle Dusty had insisted he become almost as well versed in handling the concealed firearm he was carrying as he was a weapon drawn from a conventional gunbelt.

Passing behind his back, having been prevented from availing himself of it sooner in the fighting, the redhead's right hand brought a short-barreled Merwin &

Hulbert Army Pocket revolver from the holster tucked
into the waistband of his trousers. Although it had a
double-action mechanism that removed the need to do
so, he cocked the hammer with his thumb while raising
it to shoulder height in both hands. Believing either he
or his rescuer might be the next intended target, sight-
ing quickly with the rear sight on the frame and the
large-blade foresight at the muzzle, he sent a .44-caliber
bullet between the white hard case's eyes. He was ready
to defend himself against the rest of the group, but they
all continued to run away with barely more than a backward glance at their stricken companions.

"*Gracias*, Danny!" the redhead said after the surviving would-be assailants disappeared around a corner.
"I'm right pleased you came back when you did."

"The man who came out of the back door there had a
horse," the small Oriental replied, cleaning the blade of
his sword with a handkerchief and returning it to its
bamboo-covered sheath. His English was excellent, with
a sibilant timbre that was different from the tones generally employed by the majority of Chinese.[1] "I went
after him, but he'd gone from sight by the time I got to
the corner, so I thought I'd come back to tell you about
him. What now?"

"I'll stop here and tell the law what's come off,"
Charlie replied, glancing to where the Mexican's body
gave a convulsive shudder and went limp. "Looks like
he's cashed his chips and won't be able to help us any.
You'd best get back to the governor's place as fast as
you can make it. I've a notion that the jasper Miz Freddie calls a 'civil servant' could be in *real* bad trouble,
which don't worry me a whole heap except I reckon
Uncle Dusty's going to want to ask him what brought
him here and who he was talking to. What's more, I'll be
real surprised if between us we can't sort of persuade
him all loving and gentle to tell us everything we want to
know."

1. *Danny Okasi was not Chinese. He was Japanese, a trained samurai warrior—which explains his skill at fighting in such an (to Occidental eyes) unusual fashion—and serving a family obligation by living in the United States with the Hardin, Fog, and Blaze clan as an uncle had done previously.*

1a. *Information about the uncle, Tommy Okasi, can be found in the Ole Devil Hardin and Floating Outfit series.*

4

I'M GETTING TOO *OLD* FOR DOING THIS

"It looks as if our dear friend, the civil servant, has decided to come back instead of taking the rest of the day off," Mrs. Freddie Fog commented as she and her husband were on the point of leaving the Anderson mansion at the end of a longer stay than they had anticipated. "I've never known one of them to be so eager to work."

Before the Fogs could take their departure at the conclusion of the discussion they had had with the governor, the state's attorney general had arrived for an informal visit. Knowing him to be a man whose integrity and discretion could be relied upon implicitly, as well as a friend of long standing, Freddie and Dusty had decided to inform him of the arrangements that were being made to try to produce a cure for the so-called Texas fever. On learning of the condition regarding the man who was to be brought in to protect Frank Smith while

the work was being done, he had stated that he thought
the pardon could be granted without too serious political repercussions in the event of its success. However,
they had mentioned neither their suppositions with regard to the secretary nor the activities in which their
companions were engaged.

Talking over the issue with Dusty before they left the
OD Connected ranch, possessing a justifiable mistrust
of what her British background led her to call "civil
servants,"[1] Freddie had claimed that Dell—whose position qualified him for that category in her opinion—was
the most likely prospect for any betrayal that might take
place. Nevertheless, being fair-minded, she had admitted that her supposition might prove to stem from nothing more than personal prejudice. Therefore, neither
she nor Dusty had discounted the possibility of there
being other candidates among the domestic staff at the
mansion or working in the Capitol Building who would
have similar opportunities to obtain and misuse confidential information. Accepting that they could not
achieve anything should the traitor be at the latter, they
had arranged for Hank Blaze to remain on the premises
with the means to go after a suspect using some form of
transportation, while his elder brother, Charlie, and
Danny Okasi kept watch from the street beyond the
front fence and were-ready to follow anybody who left
on foot.

On taking his departure, Edmund Dell had made an
error of deduction when failing to see Hank. Although
invited by the elderly Negro butler to go into the
kitchen for a meal or some liquid refreshments, Hank
had claimed to be suffering from the result of the previous evening's festivities in town and asked if he might
have a beer in the cool shade offered by a summer
house that offered him an unrestricted view of the front
of the mansion. This was done, and he had been able to
watch the secretary without being observed in return.

Having noticed the furtive way in which the secretary was behaving on coming through the front doors, Hank believed that the suspicions expressed by "Miz Freddie"—as his sibling and many other people referred to his aunt out of respect and fondness—could be justified. Therefore, waiting until Charlie and Danny Okasi were going after Dell, he had returned the empty beer schooner to the kitchen. In the course of an otherwise innocuous conversation with the staff, he had contrived to learn that Dell generally left in the buggy.

The Fogs' relationship with Hank had not been mentioned on their arrival at the mansion. In fact, it was implied that he was merely a hired hand accompanying them to carry out menial tasks. Making the excuse to the butler that he wanted to find out how much longer his "boss" and "Miz Freddie" would be at the mansion, so he would know whether to take care of their animals—which in truth had come only a fairly short distance from the hotel and at a leisurely pace, so had not suffered any neglect by being left ready for immediate use at the hitching rail—Hank had been taken to the governor's private office. Brought into the entrance hall, on being informed of what had taken place and the young redhead's discoveries regarding Dell, Dusty had said he should remain in some point of vantage in case somebody else left.

With the discussions and other amenities concluded, having excused themselves on the grounds that they wanted to return to their hotel and dress for the reception in the evening, Freddie and Dusty were on the point of having Hank fetched from wherever he was waiting so they could take their departure. However, their attention was drawn to the sight of Dell coming along the street.

"Maybe he found out he'd forgotten something when he got to where he's bunking down and's come back for it," the small Texan suggested, looking through the open

door across the wide expanse of a well-kept lawn fringed
by beds of flowers to where Dell was approaching the
front gates of the property along the street. "Anyways, I
don't see any sign of young Charlie or Danny coming
after him."

"That could mean, wherever he went, they must have
thought it wasn't for a harmless reason," the beautiful
woman guessed. "So they decided they'd be better employed by letting him go and following whoever he's
been to see."

"Could be he's only come back to fetch something he
forgot to take home with him," Dusty suggested, but his
voice implied no conviction in the supposition.

"It could," Freddie conceded in a tone redolent of
disbelief. "But if that was the case, I'm sure either
Henry or Danny would have come back to t—!"

Before the beautiful woman could complete her comment, there was a dramatic interruption.

Although Pampa did have his origins and spent his for-
mative years in the vicinity of the town from which he
took his sobriquet, his participation in various illicit activities had compelled him to spend the past few years
east of the Mississippi River. For some of the time, he
had been employed by a private detective agency that
lacked scruples where the handling of assignments was
concerned and did not inquire too closely into the past
of the men they hired. Having carried out similar tasks
in other cities, putting the skills he had acquired to use,
he had contrived to follow Dell without being detected.
What was more, before he had gone far, he had satisfied
himself that the red-haired young Texan was not coming
after him. Having gone only a short distance, taking notice of the furtive way in which the man he was following behaved, he was convinced that his employer was
correct in the assumptions mentioned while they were
talking in the back room at the saloon.

While hurrying along the streets, Dell had constantly glanced to his rear as if expecting to spot somebody on his trail. On a couple of occasions, in spite of the precautions that were taken to avoid detection, he caught a glimpse of Pampa. However, because he was watching specifically for the young redhead, he did not pay any more attention to the big hard case than he had in the saloon. Therefore, he arrived at the gates of the mansion without realizing he was in danger. Nor was he given an opportunity to discover how dangerously wrong his lack of awareness in this matter had been.

Having observed the way the secretary had acted just before leaving the saloon and noted where he was going, but not guessing the reason, Pampa decided to act upon the orders he was given by the man in the back room. A glance around told him everything was as he wanted. Looking through the iron railings surrounding the property and along the lengthy gravel path across the well-kept gardens, he could not see the couple who were about to leave, although the front door of the mansion was open. Nor was there anybody else either in the grounds or on the street. Satisfied upon that point, he felt sure he could carry out his task without interference. What was more, because the rest of his immediate surroundings was just as devoid of people, he stood a good chance of getting away without being seen. Upon reaching that gratifying conclusion, he drew the long-barreled Colt Cavalry Model Peacemaker from its shoulder holster.

Cocking the revolver's action with his thumb, the hard case lined it at shoulder height with both hands. Making sure of his aim, he fired. Even as the smoke of the detonated powder left the muzzle and the barrel rose to the recoil's kick, his instincts suggested that he had made the hit he wanted. Sure enough, caught in the back of the skull by the .45 bullet, Dell was pitched forward to sprawl facedown in front of the open gate.

Having seen more than one man shot in the head, Pampa was satisfied that he had prevented any chance of the betrayal he and the man who had given the orders felt sure would take place when young Blaze reported where the secretary had been and he was questioned.

Turning and starting to walk away swiftly, the hard case was on the point of replacing the Colt in its holster when he discovered that his escape might not prove as easy as he had envisaged.

Hearing the shot and watching Dell going down, Freddie and Dusty reacted promptly, albeit in different fashions.

"Henry!" the beautiful woman shouted. The word rang through the mansion and its grounds with a volume first acquired while hunting foxes in rural Leicestershire before she was compelled to leave England and kept up throughout the varied, frequently hectic and eventful, career she had had since circumstances brought her to spend the rest of her life in the United States. "Henry Blaze!"

Leaving his wife to summon assistance, the small Texan hurtled through the front door. Crossing the porch, he went to where the horses were standing. Snatching free the reins of the mount belonging to Hank, a sixteen-hand bay gelding selected from his mount at the OD Connected as being well suited for traveling a long distance and also capable of a fair turn of speed, Dusty turned it away from the hitching rail.

Letting out a yell of "Yeeagh!" as he had so often while leading Company C of the Texas Light Cavalry in surprise attacks on the Union troops in Arkansas during the War Between the States,[2] Dusty set the animal into motion. While doing so, he grabbed the low horn of the double-girthed Texas range saddle in both hands. Pulled forward, he used the momentum to help him vault and swing astride the horse's back with the deft ease that bespoke long experience in matters equestrian. Finding the stirrup irons and inserting his feet without the need to look down, aided by the sharp toes of his boots, he used his heels to induce a greater speed. While galloping along the drive, he gripped the reins in his teeth and, sitting erect, removed his jacket. Having tossed aside the garment, he retrieved the reins and looked at the motionless shape by the gate in passing. Only one glance was required to inform him that Dell would not be able to answer any questions.

Going through the gate, the small Texan did not have any difficulty in ascertaining the identity of the secretary's killer. Lined with estates similar in layout to the one he was leaving, albeit with different styles of elegant main buildings, the street stretched straight and wide for about half a mile. Much to his relief, there was only one person on it. That meant there was no danger of some harmless and innocent bystander getting caught up in the gunplay that, since the man was holding a revolver, he felt sure was unavoidable.

Although Pampa had been born and reared in the town from which he had taken his nickname, he had spent the past few years following the trade of hired killer in various big cities outside his home state. Therefore, despite having noticed the horses standing in front of the mansion while preparing to kill Dell, he had failed to take them into account as a possible threat to his safety. Always a town dweller and never having worked as a cowhand, his long absence from Texas had further caused him to forget how practically every man in the cattle-raising areas immediately thought of riding a horse rather than using one harnessed to a vehicle of some kind, when needing to go anywhere in a hurry. Therefore, it was not until he heard the drumming of rapidly approaching hooves that he realized pursuit had been started far more quickly than he had anticipated.

Glancing over his shoulder, the hard case let out a snarl of anger at the sight of the rider coming from the entrance of the property and turning the horse his way. Pampa was moving swiftly, the Hersome gaiter boots being far more suitable for walking and—if necessary— running than a cowhand's footwear would have been. For all that, he knew he could not flee at a sufficiently rapid pace to escape whatever threat was posed by the man on the fast-striding animal. Refraining from putting away the Colt, he swiveled around and brought it up. Concluding that he would have time for only one shot before the pursuer was upon him, and taking into account how the animal's head partially shielded the rider, he directed the bullet to where his instincts in such matters suggested it would do most good under the circumstances.

While riding along the path to the gate, Dusty had been too occupied with controlling the powerful, spirited, and unfamiliar horse he had borrowed to arm himself. He was about to rectify the situation when he saw the danger. Although his right hand was on the point of drawing the bone-handled Colt Civilian Model Peacemaker from its holster on the left side of his gunbelt, he realized that—fast as he undoubtedly was—he would not be able to finish the movement and prevent what he knew was coming. Proving his assessment of the situation was correct, before the weapon came clear of leather, flame spurted from the barrel of the tall man's revolver. Struck in the chest by the bullet, the horse screamed and reared, then started to go down.

The hard case at the saloon had been correct when intimating that the small Texan had not been engaged upon as many hectic and action-packed events recently as was the case throughout much of his younger days. Nevertheless, he had not allowed himself to sink into a comfortable and sedentary retirement. Although he was now accepted as being the owner of the great OD Con-

nected ranch, he still spent as much time as possible
working at various cowhand chores. Therefore, he had
lost few of the riding skills that often kept him from
death or injury while he was serving as an officer in the
Army of the Confederate States and subsequently while
the leading member of Ole Devil Hardin's legendary
floating outfit.

Feeling the horse collapsing beneath him, Dusty reacted instinctively. His left foot slid free at the stirrup
iron with the same ease its sharp toe had done while
entering. Then, as he swung it forward over the saddle
horn swiftly and dropped the reins, the right boot was
also extracted. Thrusting himself sideways, he went
clear of the crumpling and falling animal. However, as
he alighted on the street, he stumbled. In doing so, he
inadvertently saved his life. The bullet Pampa sent his
way missed by such a narrow margin that it stirred the
back of his shirt in passing.

Although aware of how near he had come to being
shot, Dusty did not allow the realization to prevent him
from controlling the loss of balance rapidly. Having
demonstrated he had lost none of his ability as a horseman, he next proved he still retained his skill at handling the matched Colts to the superlative pitch that had
earned him the sobriquet "Rio Hondo gun wizard" and
led the Comanche Indians to call him "Magic Hands."[3]
Turning at the waist the instant he had regained his
equilibrium and completing the draw with an almost
eye-baffling speed, he fetched up the Colt, his left hand
joining the right on the butt. Much as he would have
preferred to take the man alive for questioning, he
sighted in the only way he knew would meet the extreme
urgency of the situation, thumbing back the hammer as
the Colt was rising.

Already the long-barreled revolver was being turned
toward the small Texan, and even without the evidence
presented by Dell's body, he could see it was being han-

dled with a skill that precluded taking the careful aim that would be required to allow him to inflict even a merely incapacitating wound. He fired the moment he was sure of the alignment, and it was not a moment too soon. His bullet took the man in the center of the forehead, shattering through the brain and bringing instantaneous death before bursting out the back of the skull. In spite of that, the Cavalry Model Colt barked. Fortunately, the aim was just sufficiently off for Dusty to escape with nothing more than the wind of the lead disturbing his hair.

"Whooee!" the small Texan breathed as Pampa's lifeless body crashed to the street. "I'm getting too *old* for doing this sort of thing." Then he looked back to where his wife, nephew, and other people from the governor's mansion were approaching the body of the secretary. "I wonder who he went to see and how much he heard us talking about so he could tell them."

1. *How "Miz Freddie" Fog came by her mistrust of "civil servants" is told in* DECISION FOR DUSTY FOG.
2. *Details of Dusty Fog's career while serving in command of Company C, Texas Light Cavalry, during the Arkansas campaign are recorded in the Civil War Series.*
3. *Where the circumstances that led to Dusty Fog's being given the sobriquet "Magic Hands" took place is described in* THE DEVIL GUN.

5

WE CAN PICK UP A BOUNTY

"I'm sorry over the way things turned out," Charlie Blaze asserted, looking around the small group that had assembled to discuss the events of the afternoon in Matthew Anderson's study at eight o'clock that evening. "Likely I should've took off straight after that jasper instead of going to tell Danny I was figuring on doing it."

"Leave the looking back at what should or shouldn't have been done to middle class–middle management softshells who have never done anything themselves and never will. That's all *they* are good for," Freddie Fog advised soothingly. "You called the play as you saw it, and going off without letting Danny know about it would have been foolish."

"*Gracias,* ma'am," the redhead said, both relieved and pleased by being granted the support of the beauti-

ful woman for whom he had a respect exceeded only by
that he accorded his uncle Dusty.

Unlike his aunt and uncle, who were clad in formal
evening attire suitable for the reception that was taking
place in the main dining room, Charlie was dressed as
he had been in the afternoon. However, despite the governor's and the state attorney general's presence, the
slight hint of concern he had been showing while
describing his share of the events did not arise from
speaking in such exalted company. He had met both
when they were paying visits to the OD Connected
ranch and had been hunting with them on a couple of
occasions.

Eager though Dusty Fog had been to discover what
had led up to the killing of Dell, and despite having
been a successful peace officer on occasion during his
career, courtesy had required that he wait until the town
marshal arrived and took charge instead of beginning an
inquiry on his own.[1] However, they were old friends,
and as he had surmised would prove the case, he was
invited to participate. Despite all their efforts, they had
learned little that helped clear up the mysterious aspects
of the affair.

A search of Pampa's body had revealed nothing with
which he could be identified, or even lead to the place in
town where he was staying. However, the arrival of
Danny Okasi and, later, Charlie had supplied a starting
point for the investigation. The owner of the saloon, on
being interviewed, his manner suggesting he was impressed more by the presence of Dusty Fog than that of
the marshal, had said the two rooms were rented for an
indefinite period by a man who claimed they were
needed so he could carry out private interviews with
people who had information for sale about events
around the Capitol Building. He asserted that Dell and
Pampa—whose name he had overheard—had been the
only visitors. None of the other hard cases in the latter's

regular party had ever been given admittance to the rooms.

Pressed for further details and supplying them with thinly veiled reluctance, the saloon owner asserted that the man who rented the rooms was at least six feet tall and had longish black hair. He was heavily built, with somewhat sallow features most noticeable for spectacles with dark blue lens that prevented the color of his eyes from being seen, a very large nose, a huge walrus mustache, and buckteeth. Although the owner claimed that the man's voice did not offer any definite suggestion of where he had come from, except that it was most likely somewhere beyond the Mississippi River, he was always well-dressed after the Eastern riding fashion. It was a description that matched and added to the one already supplied by Danny, who had watched the man pass him on leaving by the rear door. However, the little Oriental's hope of following him had been thwarted by his quarry having a horse available and by the attack upon Charlie.

A lengthy search carried out by the marshal's deputies had located the rooming house where Pampa had been staying. However, before the peace officers arrived, his property had been removed by his surviving companions and, as was suggested by a visit to the livery stable from which they had collected their horses, apparently they had elected to leave town before they could be captured.

"How about the man who hired the room at the saloon?" Governor Anderson asked after listening to Dusty's description of the investigation.

"Nobody seems to have seen hide nor hair of him since he got away from Danny," the small Texan replied. He looked slightly more impressive and even contrived to seem completely at ease in his excellently tailored evening suit and the stiff-fronted white shirt with a high closed collar set off by a small cambric bow tie. However, although he had gone along with his wife's insistence that he wear such garments, his footwear was still sharp-toed and high-heeled black boots of cowhand style, with the uppers under the narrow legs of the trousers. "But, 'cepting Freddie won't let me be a betting man, I'd lay odds that he's still around town."

"Well, he shouldn't be hard to find," the governor asserted. "The marshal and his deputies have a pretty good description to work with."

"Why, sure," Dusty conceded.

Before any more could be said, Anderson's elderly Negro butler came into the study and approached to whisper to his employer.

"I'm afraid we're going to have to bring this to an end," the governor stated with a smile. "Melissa has sent Jacob to remind me our other guests are waiting to see us."

"Wives've a hab—!" the small Texan began, then directed a glance at his own spouse. "*Some* wives have a habit of doing things like that. Anyways, Matt, there's nothing more we can do. It's all up to the local law from here on in."

"*I'll* make sure they keep on working at it," Anderson promised grimly. "But I wish we knew why Dell went to see him."

"Could be he was listening through the wall with a glass while we were talking in here," Dusty guessed, but he did not state his belief that the town marshal would continue to carry out just as thorough an investigation without such an inducement from the governor. "Belle Boyd taught me to do it, and I reckon the lib-rad softshells could've learned the trick. It'd suit their sneaky kind of ways."[2]

"I wish I'd thought of something like that," the governor growled, willing to accept the assumptions made by the small Texan and wondering how much more information had been divulged as the result of such eavesdropping. "Not that I'd have believed he'd have the guts to do it." Then he looked from Dusty to Freddie and back, continuing, "Did *you* suspect he'd be listening to us from the beginning of our talk?"

"Let's just say I've never trusted civil servants," the beautiful woman replied. "Especially when they're lib-rad softshells like Dell. There isn't one of them who wouldn't sell his own mother if he thought he could help his 'cause' by doing it—provided he could do so believing there wouldn't be a chance of him getting caught out."

"Then he'll have told the feller we've got Frank Smith coming to try to find the cure for the Texas fever," Anderson pointed out, having no more faith than Freddie or Dusty in the integrity of the dead man and feeling just as sure he would have passed on whatever information he had contrived to obtain. "Damn it, whoever he met at the saloon will know what's going on."

"Some of it," the small Texan admitted, sounding remarkably unconcerned over the possibility. "The bunch we're up against are slick enough to figure out you'll be just as set as us cattle folks are on having a cure found for the Texas fever and would guess why you'd sent for Freddie and me to drop by, even though we're just supposed to be here as guests at your shindig. Which being, they'd have passed word for him to listen in and tell their man what was said."

"In that case," the governor said in a worried tone, "Dell will have told whoever he went to meet that Mark's going to meet Wa—the man who'll be riding shotgun on Smith."

"Only, as none of us named names, 'cepting Frank Smith, he didn't learn who we're bringing," Dusty reminded, having given a warning glance that prevented his host from completing the name of the man whose identity had not been mentioned at any time during the earlier meeting. "Nor where Mark and him're meeting up and he'll be fetching young Smith from, or where they'll be hiding up while the work's being done on finding the cure."

"Anyway," Freddie said, standing up with an air of finality. "We can't change anything that was said now, and Melissa is waiting with more patience than I would have in her shoes for us to join the rest of the party."

Taking the hint, although he was still disturbed by the thought of the information that his late secretary might have divulged, the governor led the way to the door of the study. Much to his relief, as he did not wish to attend, Charlie had already been told by his aunt that he need not accompany them. That left him at liberty to go join his brother on the visit to a part of the town they considered more suitable to their tastes and see if they might learn anything further of use. Having come to the mansion later to act as driver of the four-passenger surrey, Danny Okasi was spending the time in the servants' quarters and conducting similar inquiries to discover whether any of them could supply information about Dell, or anybody else, that might prove of assistance in preventing a further leakage of confidential matters.

On entering the much larger room on the ground floor, Freddie and Dusty found much the same kind of guests assembled as they had expected. There were members of the state legislature, even some whose political allegiances were in opposition to the governor, local businessmen, a few Army officers, and a number of ranchers, several of the latter also in cowhand-style boots as an adjunct to their otherwise formal attire. Many of the men were accompanied by their wives, and it was toward the latter that the beautiful black-haired woman gravitated after she and her husband had been taken to be introduced to those of the assemblage with whom he was not acquainted. Because of his long involvement in various aspects of ranching, Dusty found himself the center of the cattlemen. His opinion was asked about the threats to have the passage of trail herds north banned, and from the comments he heard, he realized just how seriously such a proposal would be resisted if it should be implemented.

"What do you make of those white-faced cattle that're coming in from England, Dusty?" a rancher inquired after some more discussion on what could be done in the event some form of action against allowing the passage of trail herds took place, followed by a reference to the attempt to find a cure for the Texas fever. "Herefords, they call them, don't they?"

"Why, sure," the small Texan answered. "We're raising some down to the OD Connected, and I like what I see. Top of which, Mark Counter's wrote to say he's doing the same at the MC and, going by what I heard tell, so is Tolly Maxwell in Deaf Smith County."

While speaking, Dusty became aware of a sensation he experienced only when being watched. Glancing around in casual-seeming fashion, he noticed a tall, slender, smartly dressed, and distinguished-looking guest with a neatly trimmed black beard and longish hair standing nearby and, despite apparently listening to another group of guests, gazing at him. Having been introduced earlier as Dr. Erasmus Pettigrew, who was hoping to make a study of the local varieties of wild animals while on vacation from the East, the small Texan knew he was attending as a friend brought by one of the opposition politicians. However, although continuing to look their way, the man did not offer to take any part in the conversation between the ranchers.

"That's for sure," exclaimed another cattleman, with a broad grin. "When I met him up to Cowtown a few months back, Tolly allowed he's took to them so well, he's got Deaf Smith's county seat called after them."

"What he told me," put in a third member of the group, also showing amusement since the man under discussion was well known as a practical joker with a very lively sense of humor, "he reckoned's how since that's where they come from back in England, they'd for certain sure settle down 'n' prosper near a town called Hereford."

"How're they doing, Dusty?" inquired the rancher who had raised the subject.

"They put on beef a whole heap better than long-horns and seem to be able to fend for themselves un-tended on the range pretty near as well, although I don't know how they'd stand up to the weather further north in a bad winter," the small Texan answered, still watching Dr. Pettigrew surreptitiously. However, the scrutiny to which he himself had been subjected was brought to an abrupt end, as if the other had become aware that it was noticed. "If they do that, could be they're what's needed to push up our profit by bringing in more money per carcass."

On entering his room in the town's best hotel shortly before midnight, although the clerk at the reception desk had not mentioned such would be the case, the guest who had been introduced at the governor's recep-tion as Dr. Erasmus Pettigrew showed no surprise at finding that somebody was there. The visitor had taken a room farther along the corridor on checking in the day after the doctor arrived, and they had never given any indication of even being acquainted.

"How have you found things around town?" Petti-grew inquired, starting to remove his high hat.

"Quiet enough," replied the unannounced visitor. Ex-cept for height and build, his appearance did not match the description that had been supplied to Dusty Fog and the town marshal. Nevertheless, his voice was that of the unseen occupant in the back room of the saloon where the secretary had been told to report with whatever in-formation regarding the so-called Texas fever was gath-ered. "The local John Laws managed to find where

Pampa was staying, but that bunch he had working for him got there first and cleared it out."

"Did he have anything that could lead them to *us?*" Pettigrew asked while hanging his hat and frock coat in the wardrobe.

"Not a thing," the visitor claimed with confidence. "In fact, he didn't know even where we were staying. From what I heard around town, the rest of them got out of town as soon as they'd taken his gear. So we'll have to get some fresh help for the rest of the contract. How did your night go?"

"Well, not that it surprises me, being the stupid bastard that he was, going by all you've told me, but Dell was *wrong,*" Pettigrew announced. His accent was that of a well-educated New Englander. "Counter isn't going to meet whoever they're bringing in at Brownsville, but I know where they're getting together."

"I'm pleased to hear it," replied the visitor. "Because I've learned who it is they're sending for to help them and where he's coming from, and I felt sure he wouldn't be going all the way across to Brownsville to meet Counter. Once I've found out what kind of help we can get when we go to where they are meeting, we can fix it so he never reaches it alive."

"They'll just send somebody else to fetch Smith when he doesn't meet Counter," Pettigrew pointed out, looking as intently at the other man as he had been doing while standing near Dusty Fog at the reception.

"So we'll get more money out of them for finding out who it is," the visitor stated, showing no sign of being in any way surprised or put out by the scrutiny. "Then we'll follow that one to Smith and kill them both when they meet up. By playing it that way, we'll get a double pay-off."

"How come?" Pettigrew inquired.

"It's the same as with Dell," the visitor answered. "When we get him killed, we can pick up a bounty from

somebody else as well as these fellers who're hiring us to
stop a cure being found for the Texas fever."

"I don't see how can we get paid off for Dell," Pettigrew claimed.

"Easy enough," the visitor asserted. "With the proof
we've got to show that we've had it done, we'll get the
cash put on the lavender boy from the folks in Fort
Worth who want his hide nailed to the wall."

"So you told me this afternoon," Pettigrew pointed
out. "But what did the bunch who've hired us say about
it happening?"

"I told them that I'd reason to think he was going to
sell us—and *them*—out to the governor, so they said I'd
acted for the best," the other man answered. "Anyways,
it's much the same with the feller who Fog's bringing in
to guard Smith. There's money to be made out of killing
him."

"That's true. You said Dell told you he's wanted by
the law."

"Turns out lavender boy was right about *that*, but the
bounty gets paid only if he's fetched in alive."

"We don't want to waste time and attract attention to
ourselves by getting mixed up with any kind of deal like
that," Pettigrew declared.

"And we don't need to be," the other man replied.
"I'm not thinking of handing him over to the law.
There's a feller down to Mexico who'll pay well to have
him dead. One way or another, this is going to prove a
real profitable chore for us."

---

1. *Some information about Dusty Fog's career as a peace officer is given
in* QUIET TOWN, THE MAKING OF A LAWMAN; THE TROU-
BLE BUSTERS; DECISION FOR DUSTY FOG; CARDS AND
COLTS; THE CODE OF DUSTY FOG; ARIZONA RANGE WAR
ARIZONA GUN LAW; THE TOWN TAMERS *and* THE SMALL
TEXAN.
2. *Some events in the career of Belle "the Rebel Spy" Boyd, a "secret
agent" for the Confederate States and later a member of the U.S. Secret*

Service, are recorded in MISSISSIPPI RAIDER; THE COLT AND THE SABRE; THE REBEL SPY; BLOODY BORDER; RENEGADE; THE BAD BUNCH; SET A-FOOT; TO ARMS! TO ARMS! IN DIXIE!; THE SOUTH WILL RISE AGAIN; THE QUEST FOR BOWIE'S BLADE; Part Eight, "Affair of Honour," J. T.'S HUNDREDTH; THE REMITTANCE KID; THE WHIP AND THE WAR LANCE; *and* Part Five, "The Butcher's Fiery End," J. T.'S LADIES.

2a. *Having learned about the trick of employing a glass tumbler held to the ear and placed against a wall as an aid to eavesdropping from "Miz Freddie," Dusty Fog's grandson, Alvin Dustine, made use of it on at least two of his assignments as a member of Company Z, Texas Rangers, in the Prohibition era.* See CAP FOG, TEXAS RANGER, MEET MR. J. G. REEDER *and* RAPIDO CLINT STRIKES BACK.

6

HE WANTS BOTH HANDS
CUT OFF

"Hold it up!"

Being slightly ahead of his companion as they traveled west along a trail leading from Hereford, seat of Deaf Smith County, Texas, toward the border with New Mexico late on a pleasant mid-June afternoon, the taller of the two riders was able to see over the rim they were ascending before the other was in a position to do so. Stopping his horse as he spoke, his tone was more that of a command to an employee than a suggestion for the benefit of a friend.

"What's up, Monte?" inquired the second horseman, who was an inch shorter and more thickset, as he duplicated the action by reining his mount to a halt.

"There's a feller coming this way," Albert "Monte" Parker answered, and opened the right-side pouch on his saddle. Raising the field glasses he extracted, he fo-

cused them and went on with satisfaction, "Now, that's
what I call real *lucky!*"

"You mean it's *him* already?" Joel Daly asked, moving forward until he, too, could look at the rider approaching from the west along the trail.

"It's *him!*" the taller rider confirmed in a voice that
was assured and satisfied, having been given a description—but no name—and told how the man he was hired
to kill could be located. Like his companion, he had not
expected the meeting to come so soon. Still looking, he
continued, "Clothes're right, including the black gloves
I was told he'd be wearing no matter what else he had
on."

"He's too far off for me to see 'em," the shorter man
declared, having no such aid to vision. Then he glanced
at his companion. "I wonder who it is's wants him dead,
'n' why."

"All I need to know is I—*we're*—being paid good
money to do it," Parker stated with a scowl that rendered his unprepossessing features even less pleasant.
His response was caused by having a similar interest in
the subject and a dislike for being unable to display
superior knowledge to somebody he regarded as no
more than an unimportant and disposable hired hand.
"One thing I learned real early was *never* to get nosy
over who's doing the paying."

Having a similarly wolfish look to their features, the
two men wore the attire generally associated with cowhands from the Northern cattle-raising states. However,
the clothing they had on notwithstanding—even without
suggestions to the contrary offered by their conversation—to range-wise eyes, neither was likely to have any
extensive knowledge of the everyday tasks performed by
that hard-riding, hardworking, harder-playing fraternity.
Rather, they showed indications, unmistakable to anybody who knew the West, that they earned their living
from a willingness to use the Colt Peacemaker each was

carrying in a low-tied holster on his gunbelt—that of Daly supplemented by a sheathed hunting knife on the left—and Winchester Model of 1873 rifles in the boots of their single-girthed saddles. Although each rig had a bedroll on the cantle, there was no coiled rope strapped to either's horn. Nor did the pair consider such an item, indispensable though it was to a cowhand, to be a necessary aid. They were, in fact, engaged upon a line of work that was ages old. Professional killers had been used since earliest times and, human nature being what it is, probably always will be.[1]

"I was thinking there's sometimes money to be got from knowing who's doing the hiring," Daly explained, his unshaven face sullen. " 'Specially when you know it's not the jasper who's given you the chore and it's got to be done like *this* has."

"Likely whoever's paying us to make wolf bait of this jasper wants to know it's been done afore he hands over the money," Parker guessed, realizing which aspect of the affair had prompted the second comment. "Only, he figures it wouldn't be healthy in more ways than one to have the body fetched in for him to look over."

"So we could take everything the jasper's toting on him, or his hosses and clothes, seeing it's knowed what he's riding and wearing. But hell's teeth, Monte, what kind of feller is it's wants blue windows put into him?"

"How'd you mean?"

"You *know* how I mean! I can see why he'd want the body hid so it don't get found, but he wants both hands cut off 'n' took to him. A man must have a whole heap of hate in him to ask for *that!*"

"Could be. Only, which being, I sure's hell don't want to get somebody that hate-filled riled up at *me* 'cause he figures I'm pushing my nose into his private doings, 'stead of just taking my pay and 'tending to my own affairs."

"Sure," Daly grunted. "Only, wanting things done the

way he does, could be that feller's deck's shy a few cards. Which being, I'm none too happy with the notion of working for a crazy man."

"Don't let *that* worry you none," the taller rider advised grimly. " 'Cause the fellers I—*we're*—dealing with's sane enough no matter what it might be with whoever he's getting paid by, and *he's* one man I sure don't figure on riling."

Having had similar misgivings on hearing the most unusual proof of success demanded by the man who wanted the killing done, Parker had felt it inadvisable to handle the task alone, and had negotiated the point through an intermediary. What was more, even without the bizarre terms imposed, he always had a disinclination to take unnecessary chances and preferred to have the odds in his favor. Therefore, he had asked his companion along because nobody else with whom he had worked previously was available at such short notice. However, despite having for a second time changed an "I" to a "we," he did not regard Daly as a partner. Nor had he any intention of sharing the payment once the task was completed.

"I'm right *pleased* to hear it!" Daly said, but without any great conviction, as his spurs nudged against the ribs of his horse. "Anyways, we ain't going to be long over finishing this chore."

"Stay put, goddamn it!" Parker commanded savagely. "What the hell do you reckon you're doing?"

"Going to earn our pay," the shorter hired killer answered, but he restrained his mount before he could ride past his companion. His manner became challenging as he inquired, "That's what we've come out here for, ain't it?"

"Yeah," the taller man admitted, and put a less hostile timbre into his voice as he continued. "Only, there ain't no sense in making things harder than we have to, Joel. No matter what I was told by S—I got told, that jasper could know somebody's gunning for him and be on the lookout for it. Even if he ain't, he's likely to watch anybody riding toward him real careful."

"Uh-huh!" the shorter man grunted. Having no desire to provoke a confrontation with his companion, whom he knew to be quick-tempered and suspected was better with a gun than himself, he contrived to look mollified even though he was far from feeling it. "Do you *know* that jasper out there?"

"Like I told you, I wasn't given no name," Parker answered, and gestured with the aid to vision he had used. "I can't bring to mind ever having seen him afore."

"Give me the glasses," Daly suggested, holding out his grubby right hand. "I might have, and it could help if we know exactly who and what we're up against."

"Here," the taller hired gun said, appreciating the wisdom behind the request and wishing he had drawn the conclusion first.

Accepting and lining up the field glasses, being equally disinclined to take chances and willing to obey orders only if he was satisfied they would produce the desired results without undue danger to himself, Daly studied the intended victim. He needed only one glance to decide that he could not make an identification. Nevertheless, despite the considerable distance that separated them, he conceded that his companion had been right when claiming they could be up against somebody it would prove most unwise to treat with other than the greatest caution.

However, there was nothing about the appearance of the approaching man to suggest why the unknown employer wanted him dead, or had felt it necessary to issue the bizarre instructions for receiving proof of his demise. On the other hand, to anybody who had been around the range country as long as Daly, there was

little doubt about the origins of the intended victim—
even without hearing him speak.

Clearly tall, perhaps a couple of inches over six feet,
the rider was as lean as a steer raised in the greasewood
country and, even so far away, gave the impression of
being just as whang-leather tough. Tanned by long exposure to the elements, the clean-shaven face—framed by
neatly trimmed sideburns of reddish-brown hair that
had recently been barbered—was too rugged to be
termed handsome. Nevertheless, while it almost certainly displayed only such emotions as he wanted to be
seen, its lines were indicative of strength of will and
intelligence.

The suggestions of origins started with a low-
crowned, wide-brimmed black hat steamed and molded
into the style most favored by Texans. Less indicative,
except that Daly remembered having seen something
similar worn by Marvin Eldridge "Doc" Leroy in the
days when the Wedge trail crew was one of many driving
herds of half-wild longhorn cattle to the railroad in
Kansas,[2] was the rider's unfastened brown coat. Its right
side was stitched back to leave unimpeded access to a
staghorn-handled Colt Civilian Model Peacemaker,
which was butt forward in a form-fitting "Missouri Skin-
Tite" holster attached to a broad black gunbelt buckled
horizontally around his waist instead of sloping down to
the right side. While not a rig frequently seen, it was a
way of wearing a revolver favored by men who wished to
foster the belief that they were very fast with a gun—or
were.

Buttoned at the neck, the intended victim's blue flannel shirt had a black string bow tie. They and his yellow-
ish-brown Nankeen trousers were such as might have
been worn by anybody engaged on some form of the
ranching business in any of the cattle-raising states.
However, the latter were tucked into black Wellington
leg boots, with Kelly spurs on the heels and decorated

by the five-pointed-star motif that was practically obliga-
tory for a man born and making his living on the open
ranges of Texas.[3] The black gloves he wore were not
heavy work gauntlets, but the kind frequently used by
professional gamblers who had a need to ensure that
their hands remained soft and supple.

The saddle upon which the man was seated with the
easy grace of one who spent much time riding, his
gloved left hand holding the split-end reins in a seemingly negligent fashion, was yet another sign of his connection with the Lone Star State. Although somewhat
more fancily carved than one intended for rough work
on the range, low of horn and double-girthed, it was
designed to cope with the needs of cowhands who took
pride in hanging on to whatever they roped, be it a
steer, cow, calf, bull, horse, or man. A coiled manila
rope was strapped to the left side of the horn and, beneath his near leg, a rifle of some kind—almost certainly a repeater rather than a single-shot model—rode
in a saddle boot with its butt pointing to the rear to
facilitate easy withdrawal on dismounting. The big blue
roan gelding between his knees and the similarly
equipped, equally large, blaze-faced bay—to the cantle
of whose saddle was attached a bulky bedroll and war
bag wrapped in a tarpaulin cover to protect them from
the elements—were fine animals, albeit more suited to
long traveling at a good speed than the agility required
for dealing with half-wild and often fractious cattle.

Having examined the approaching would-be victim,
Daly next studied the terrain between them. The scrutiny did not fill him with enthusiasm, or lead him to
think the task was a sinecure. The top of the rim was
completely bare, and even with the sun sinking toward
the western horizon, any attempt to fire over it would
result in whoever did so being skylined more promi-
nently than he cared to contemplate. While there was
some cover on the slope at the other side, none of it was

close enough to the trail to guarantee that the comparatively short-ranged Winchester rifles he and Parker carried would make a certain hit. Should they open fire and miss, they were unlikely to be granted a second chance. Unless electing to make a fight, even leading the bay, the Texan—as Daly now designated him—was sufficiently well mounted to turn and outrun their horses. What was more, once alerted, he would make sure that he did not present another such easy opportunity.

However, about half a mile away, there was a small stream that needed to be forded by anybody using the trail. This struck Daly as being a much more suitable proposition than crossing anywhere closer at hand. Trees and bushes coated its banks on either side, offering a variety of hiding places. The problem was how to get there without being observed. Much as it went against the grain to admit that his companion was right again, he conceded that going forward on horseback was not the answer. Even if the Texan was not expecting trouble, he had an alert appearance that warned he instinctively maintained a close watch on his surroundings at all times and, unless he differed from the majority of people who needed to travel on the open ranges of the West, would keep a wary eye on anybody approaching him.

"Well!" Parker growled, breaking in upon his companion's train of thought. "Do you know the son of a bitch?"

"I've never seen him afore," Daly confessed reluctantly, surrendering the field glasses in response to an impatient gesture from their owner. "He sure looks like he knows which end the bullets come out of a gun, though."

"Was you thinking of riding up 'n' calling him out like you was in some fancy Louisiana duel, so he's got a chance to use one?" the taller hired killer inquired sarcastically, despite agreeing with his partner's assessment.

"No!" Daly answered, his voice becoming surly. "It's just that I don't reckon we should make it any easier for him than we can help."

"I'll go along with you on *that*," Parker conceded, forcing his mount to move backward until well beyond the top of the rim. Dismounting, he drew his Winchester from its saddle boot and glanced about him. "We'll leave the hosses tied to that bush, sneak down to the stream, and lay for him. I don't take any too kind' to walking that far, but we'll be able to ride coming back."

Carrying out the instructions and arming himself with his rifle, Daly followed his companion over the rim and down the gentle slope at the other side. Having crawled across the top on their stomachs, they rose and adopted a crouching posture when they thought it was safe to do so. Then they descended more swiftly from one piece of cover to another. All the time, whether advancing or pausing briefly in concealment, they kept a careful watch on their intended victim.

Crossing some open ground about a hundred and fifty yards from their destination, the pair flushed a flock of bobwhite quail. Dropping flat immediately, they lay for a few seconds completely immobile. On raising their heads cautiously, what they saw came as a relief. For one thing, the birds had gone at an angle along the slope instead of downward where they could be scared into flying again. Even more important, the Texan showed no sign of either having been disturbed by the frightened quail or even noticing them. Instead, he was continuing to ride at the same unhurried pace along the trail. Satisfied it could be done without being detected, the pair resumed their interrupted advance.

"That's better!" Parker breathed on arriving at the first of the bushes fringing the stream.

"Yeah!" Daly agreed just as quietly, also straightening

up. "I thought he'd get spooked for sure when you scared up them goddamned bobwhites."

"They was closer to *you* than *me!*" the taller hired killer claimed, despite both men having been equally at fault. However, as he wanted to keep the peace between them until after the job was over, he went on in a blatantly magnanimous fashion. "Anyways, Joel, there wasn't no harm done. He never saw us."

"I'll take the left side," Daly stated rather than suggested, nodding to the bushes in the appropriate direction.

"Sure," Parker agreed, concluding that there was no advantage of additional safety offered by the undergrowth on one side of the trail or the other.

Going their separate ways, but each contriving to keep watching where his companion was positioned, the pair selected routes that offered them a choice of hiding places and an unrestricted field of fire at the wheel-rutted open space between them. Unfortunately, the trail bent in a fashion that prevented either from seeing as far ahead as the stream. However, neither considered this too much of a threat to the success of their ambush. Not only could they hear their intended victim approaching, but the curve also meant that he would have just as limited a range of vision and no such audible guidance to their presence.

Sure enough, even though the pair could not see the rider, the sound of hooves came to their ears. The horses were moving at a steady walk, and soon it was obvious that they had reached the stream. After the horses were allowed to pause and drink, the crossing was carried out in a similar unhurried fashion. However, on reaching dry land, the animals were brought to a halt. Then leather began to creak, and the hired killers concluded that the rider had dismounted.

"Do you reckon he's stopped to bed down for the

night?" Daly hissed after about a minute had elapsed
without the approach being resumed.

"He could have," Parker replied. Aware that the trail
was sometimes well used, he went on, "We'd best go
take a look. Somebody might come along if we leave it
until later."

"They could at that," Daly admitted. "Anyways, I
wouldn't fancy trying to sneak up on him through this
stuff in the dark."

Deciding that the undergrowth was much thicker on
his side of the trail, which was the reason he had picked
it when expecting nothing more than to wait in ambush,
the shorter hired killer crossed and joined his companion. Once again employing all the stealth they could
manage, they advanced until able to see the stream.
What met their gaze came as something of a shock.
Although the horses were standing in plain view on the
bank, securely hitched to a sturdy sapling, at first neither could locate any sign of their would-be victim.
Then the sound of whistling came to their ears. It drew
their attention to where the black boots, around which
the Nankeen trousers were hanging, showed from beneath and beyond a large and thick bush about the
height of a tall man. Jabbing an elbow into Daly's ribs,
Parker pointed with the barrel of his rifle to where the
black gunbelt and its staghorn-handled revolver were
hanging over a convenient branch.

Both the hired killers drew the same conclusion from
what they saw.

Each concluded that their task had been simplified
and, in fact, rendered completely safe.

"He's going to wish he'd took his shit out in the
open," Parker declared sotto voce, raising the Winchester to his right shoulder.

"Yeah," Daly agreed just as quietly, also bringing up
and starting to sight along the barrel of his rifle. Satisfied that the forty-grain powder charge in the cartridges

would send the bullets through the foliage and into the concealed man with little loss of velocity, he continued with a savage grin, "The stupid son of a bitch's got hisself caught with his pants down and no mistake."

"Stop talking and get the bastard," the taller hired killer ordered, tightening his right forefinger on the trigger.

1. An example of how some modern professional killers operate is given in THE PROFESSIONAL KILLERS.
2. We do not claim that Marvin Eldridge "Doc" Leroy was the originator of wearing a jacket adapted in such a fashion as an aid to making a fast draw, but our records establish that his were always converted that way. Information about his earlier career can be found in QUIET TOWN; Part Five, "The Hired Butcher," THE HARD RIDERS; Part Three, "The Invisible Winchester," OLE DEVIL'S HANDS AND FEET; Part Five, "A Case of Infectious Plumbeus veneficium," THE FLOAT-ING OUTFIT; Part Three, "Monday Is a Quiet Day," THE SMALL TEXAN; Part Two, "Jordan's Try," THE TOWN TAMERS; RE-TURN TO BACKSIGHT; Part Six, "Keep Good Temper Alive," J. T.'S HUNDREDTH; *and the Waco Series. How he achieved his ambition to become a qualified doctor is told in* DOC LEROY, M.D.
2a. The Wedge acted as a contract trail crew for those ranchers who had too few cattle to consider making up and delivering a herd to Kansas individually a viable prospect. They make guest appearances in QUIET TOWN, TRIGGER FAST; Part One, "To Separate Innocence From Guilt," MORE J. T.'S LADIES; *and* GUN WIZARD. *They also star in their own right in* BUFFALO ARE COMING!, WEDGE COMES TO ARIZONA;, *and* ARIZONA RANGE WAR; ARIZONA GUN LAW.
2b. Some information about the events that led up to Texans' taking trail herds to the railroad in Kansas can be found in GOODNIGHT'S DREAM; FROM HIDE AND HORN; SET TEXAS BACK ON HER FEET; *and* THE HIDE AND TALLOW MEN.
2c. How such trail herds were handled is described in TRAIL BOSS.
3. Another example of how clothing could identify a man as a Texan is given in Case One, "Roan Marrett's Son," ARIZONA RANGER.

7

WHERE THE HELL'S HE GOT TO?

In echo to the shot discharged by Monte Parker, Joel Daly opened fire.

Twigs and leaves flew in all directions under the withering hail of lead sent from the muzzles of the two repeaters being operated as fast as the men holding them could work the lever-action mechanisms. Although there was no sound from beyond the bush and the boots still continued to stand with the trousers hanging around them, the blue roan and the bay, whinnying in alarm, showed signs of restlessness. Held by the reins fastened to the saplings, they were prevented from running away despite the fright they had received. However, although they remained in view, the hired killers were too preoccupied to notice that there was something missing from the saddle of the animal the Texan had been riding.

There was no longer a rifle in the saddle boot.

Regardless of there being nothing to suggest such was the case, and convinced that anybody squatting or even standing behind the bush would not have had a chance of being missed by at least some of the lead sent that way, Daly darted forward. He was not only eager to obtain proof of success, but he wanted to have first pick of whatever their victim was carrying. When he peered through the bullet-ruptured foliage, all the color drained from his face.

"Monte!" the hired killer croaked.

"What's up?" Parker demanded, having followed at a slower pace in case the Texan should still be capable of resistance, and ready to shoot down his companion when satisfied they had carried out their mission successfully.

"Y-y—!" Daly gasped, being so surprised by the discovery he had made that he could not decide upon a positive response to it. "You'd best come and take a look!"

"What the hell's *wrong?*" Parker demanded, striding more quickly until alongside his companion. "Anybody'd think you've never seen a dead 'n' af—!"

The words died away as the taller hired killer became aware of what had caused the consternation being shown by his companion.

"The bastard ain't *there!*" Daly announced, a statement that was unnecessary as far as the other man was concerned.

"I can see *that!*" Parker snarled, staring in something close to horror at the unoccupied Nankeen trousers and Wellington leg boots that had helped with what was clearly a well-planned deception. Then his head jerked up and he stared around wildly, exclaiming, "Where the hell's he got to?"

"Throw those rifles away pronto if you want to stay alive long enough to see two seconds from now!"

Originating at some distance from the bush where the

firing had been directed, the order was given in a drawl
that proved Daly and Parker were correct in deducing
the intended victim was from Texas. The order was uttered before Daly could try to answer the question
asked by Parker. What was more, its wording and timbre warned that the speaker was not merely making a
polite request backed by a threat he would refrain from
putting into effect. Although the broad black gunbelt
with the staghorn-handled Colt Civilian Model Peacemaker in its Missouri Skin-Tite holster was still hanging
in plain view on the branch, he was sure to be holding
the rifle that was no longer in his saddle boot ready for
instant use.

A rapid exchange of worried glances passed between
the two hired killers. While neither could guess what
their fate might be if they surrendered, there was no
doubt in their minds over what would happen should
they offer resistance. Each was aware that a concerted
effort might allow one to locate and shoot the Texan,
but was equally certain that it would in all probability be
at the cost of the other's life. Therefore, as neither was
willing to make the sacrifice on behalf of his companion
and did not doubt the same sentiments applied where
the other was concerned, both concluded that they had
no other choice and obeyed.

"Now follow them with your gunbelts!" the still-hid-
den Texan commanded after the Winchester rifles had
been tossed aside and without giving either hired killer
an opportunity to look around. "Do it *real* slow and *left*-
handed!"

Yielding to the inevitable, Parker and Daly reached
for their gunbelts in the manner demanded by the unseen speaker. While fumbling awkwardly at the buckles,
trying to delay the removal as long as possible in the
hope that some opportunity to draw the revolver—or, in
the case of the shorter of the pair, the hunting knife—
would be presented, they heard a rustling of the foliage

from the direction in which the voice originated. Slowly turning their heads, they received their first view at close quarters of the man they had been hired to kill.

Under different circumstances, the pair might have found the appearance presented by the Texan incongruous and even amusing. Showing his shortish reddish-brown hair to be naturally wavy, the black Stetson was hanging by its fancy *barbiquejo* chin strap on his shoulders. He had discarded the coat, and this was not the full extent of his missing garments. Using the trousers and boots to help the deception that had lulled his intended killers into a potentially disastrous sense of false security left him clad below the waist in long-legged red flannel underpants and white woollen socks. However, there was nothing in the least likely to give cause for levity about his grim visage. Rather, it gave a warning that he was ready, willing, and supremely confident he could enforce his wishes as far as the circumstances demanded.

The belief that the would-be victim was armed received instant verification.

Held at shoulder height in hands still covered by black leather gloves, the rifle was directed at a point exactly between Parker and Daly. Nor did either think this was an error on the part of the Texan. They knew that, if required, it could be turned toward one or the other of them with equal facility. Being handled with an ease suggesting competence in its use, it was a weapon of excellent quality. The metal was deep blue as a result of much careful polishing during manufacture, and the woodwork had the patina of best walnut. There was a magazine tube running the full length below the octagonal barrel, but it had only a small wooden foregrip and neither the trigger guard nor loading-lever ring that had characterized the products of the Winchester Repeating Arms Company since their predecessors were sold as

the "Volcanic" and the "Henry." A closer look would
have established that it also lacked a trigger.

The pair of hired killers were too filled with consternation over the unanticipated turn of events to notice
how the weapon differed from the norm. Even if they
had seen the apparent lack of usual fittings, neither
would have concluded that it rendered the rifle harmless and intended merely to help carry out a bluff. Each
was convinced that the weapon could and would be used
with deadly effect at the slightest provocation.

Knowing he would have killed the would-be attackers
on the spot but without making his presence known
first, Parker did not care for the conclusions he was
drawing over being disarmed instead of shot down immediately. Clearly the Texan wanted to take them alive
so they could be questioned, and he suspected that the
desire for information might lead to using painful meth-
ods to extract it. Even if the motive was merely to make
them prisoners and—having handed them over to the
nearest peace officers—allow the law to take its course,
their position might not be a great deal better. The intermediary who had hired them would be disinclined to
rely upon their keeping quiet about him voluntarily, and
was sufficiently ruthless to take steps to ensure their
silence.

Unbuckling his gunbelt while reaching these unpalatable conclusions, Parker saw a possible way out of the
dilemma. A quick glance to his left informed him that
Daly had not yet duplicated his actions. An equally
rapid gaze in the other direction satisfied him that,
while there was an element of risk involved, the scheme
offered a better chance of survival than allowing himself
to be taken prisoner. With the decision reached, he
swung and tossed the liberated rig forward, trying to
give the impression that his only thought was to surren-
der.

"*Get* him, Joel!" Parker yelled the moment he opened his hand.

While speaking, the taller hired killer lunged away from his companion. He hoped that he would cause Daly to react instinctively by trying to draw and that, thinking the discarding of his own handgun made him the lesser threat, the Texan would ignore him for long enough to let him achieve his purpose. Completely indifferent to whether his behavior caused his companion to be killed, he reached out his right hand swiftly to close it around the staghorn grips of the Colt on the gunbelt left behind by their intended victim as additional bait for the trap into which they had fallen.

Bringing the revolver from the Missouri Skin-Tite rig without difficulty and starting to turn toward the Texan, Parker curled his thumb around the hammer and his forefinger entered the trigger guard. On doing so, he made two discoveries that his instincts warned caused the weapon to be very different from any other Colt Peacemaker he had handled. First, the spur of the hammer had been reduced in size, smoothed, and set lower than usual. Second, the forefinger failed to find what he expected to be there. Startled by the realization that the weapon upon which his scheme depended had been modified in such a fashion, he could not prevent himself from hesitating and glancing downward.

The spontaneous actions proved to be the last mistakes of his misspent life.

Having been keeping both men under observation, the Texan had noticed the glances taken by the taller of them. A shrewd judge of human nature, he had already concluded that Daly was the less dangerous. Making a correct deduction of what was being contemplated even as the lunge was commenced, he was swinging the barrel of his weapon in the appropriate direction.

Nor did the absence of a lever and trigger guard prevent the Texan from being able to deal with the situation. While bearing some resemblance to the products of Oliver Winchester's factory at New Haven, Connecticut, his weapon was a Colt New Lightning Magazine rifle. It had a "trombone" slide action designed from patents taken out by Doctor William H. Elliot, even before having been modified to meet his special needs, and its operation was different from that required by its better-known and much-longer-established competitors in the repeating rifle market.

Before his revolver could be turned upon him, the Texan, aware that the way it was loaded made it even more dangerous than would be a standard type of bullet, proved just how effective the Colt rifle could be in hands as skillful as his own. Instead of moving his right forefinger from where it was curled with its mates around the wrist of the modified "pistol-grip" stock, he gave a sharp thrust forward with his left hand on the foregrip. Although there was no trigger to press, a sharp crack sounded and flame lanced briefly from the muzzle. Propelled by forty grains of prime du Pont black powder, the expelled .44-caliber bullet had the flattened tip that was a necessary safety precaution for use in a magazine tube; a pointed end might cause an accidental detonation if jolted against the percussion cap in the base of the preceding cartridge. This gave the otherwise comparatively low-powered round—which could also be used in the Colt "Frontier" Model Peacemaker revolver without the danger of bursting the metal through overloading—an increased effectiveness over the distance at which it was being used.

Even as the lead passed through Parker's forehead, emerging at the back of his skull in a spray of splintered bone and pulped brain, the intended victim snapped the foregrip back and forward once more. During the brief interim between the movements a cavity appeared on top of the rifle's frame to allow the spent cartridge case to be tossed into the air through it before being closed again. While this was happening, apparently of its own volition, the exposed hammer moved to fully cocked and snapped down again. For a second time, the mechanism having replenished the chamber from the magazine tube perhaps even more quickly than would have been possible using a lever-action Winchester, another shot was discharged. It followed its predecessor with a similar accuracy. Although unnecessary, it added to the lethal damage already inflicted and helped throw Parker's lifeless body over in a backward sprawl. Then, showing the same kind of speed, the Texan caused the second empty case to be ejected as he started to turn his attention to the shorter hired killer. However, despite taking the precaution of aligning the sights, he did not complete the wrist movement required to send off the replacement bullet.

Daly had just finished unbuckling his gunbelt when his companion yelled. Although it was not yet released, and dangled by his side, he realized that he was in no position to respond with the speed his instincts warned were required to handle the latest development. Nor, seeing the deadly and effective speed with which their intended victim was reacting to the threat, did he attempt to carry out the suggested "getting." Instead, he spun around and, allowing the gunbelt to trail behind him like the tail of a frightened coyote, raced away as fast as his legs would carry him. Although the rifle was turned in his direction, it did not speak. However, expecting at any moment to feel lead slamming into him, he continued to run at the best speed he could manage through the bushes and trees. He did not slow down until he was halfway up the slope.

Having looked back and, with relief, found there was no sign of the Texan, the surviving hired killer paused just long enough to return the gunbelt to its usual position. Then he resumed the ascent at an only slightly slower pace, repeatedly glancing over his shoulder to satisfy himself that he still was not being pursued. By the time he reached the rim, he was reassured upon this point. Going to where the horses were still standing tethered to the bush, he began to unfasten the reins of his mount and gave thought to his immediate future.

"Try to get me killed so's you could escape, would you, you stinking son of a bitch?" Joel Daly growled, looking with more anger than revulsion at the body he had uncovered. "Well, it's *you's* got made wolf bait, and I hope you rot in hell!"

Releasing Monte Parker's horse as well as his own, the hired killer had taken another look to the west and made certain the Texan was not pursuing him. On the point of riding away, being almost broke as the result of a run of bad-luck gambling, he had hoped to improve the situation by returning to Parker. Concluding that he could sell his dead companion's belongings, he realized there could be another way of obtaining money. Having taken the precaution of learning where the payment would be made before accepting the offer from Parker, but without guessing that the information was supplied only because it was intended that he should not be allowed to live and go there, he would be able to collect the full amount for himself if he completed the task they had tried and failed.

Remaining out of sight beyond the rim, when the once more fully-dressed Texan had come into view, Daly had needed only a single glance to convince him that his notion was fraught with difficulties and danger. Not only was the man riding the blue roan gelding with a noticeably increased wariness, but the repeating rifle was now resting across his knees in a position of instant readiness. It was apparent that, even after nightfall, he would remain constantly on the alert and be even harder to approach undetected than appeared to be the case when they were starting to stalk him. Furthermore, once darkness descended, he would have sufficient knowledge and ability to ensure he was not located. In fact, if he suspected he was being followed, he would be able to take even more effective measures to protect himself.

Never one to take the slightest risk that could be avoided, Daly was about to ride away when he noticed what could offer another solution to his shortage of cash. The possibility was suggested by his having reminded himself that he could still sell Parker's property and wishing the weapons had not been lost to him as a result of his flight. Taking out the field glasses, he assured himself that he was correct in his assumption. Both their discarded Winchesters and his companion's gunbelt were hanging on the saddle of the second horse. However, the Texan had not brought along the corpse. Despite suspecting that all the cash and other valuables had been taken from it, as he would have done himself given the opportunity, the hired killer had realized how he might still benefit from the unusual conditions demanded by whoever had employed them to prove they had carried out their task.

Withdrawing to a safe distance and finding a place of concealment, Daly had watched the Texan disappear along the trail. Then, cursing the fading light, but grateful that nobody else had put in an appearance, he had ridden as quickly as he could to the scene of the thwarted attack. Finding the body of his companion had been easy. He had concluded that the man they had hoped to kill intended to report the matter to the sheriff of Deaf Smith County on arriving at Hereford and allow the peace officers to collect it. Covered by leaves and branches, its wolfskin jacket hanging above it to scare off scavenging wild creatures such as coyotes and turkey buzzards, it had been lying where it had fallen.

"You'll be more use to me *dead* than you would've been was you alive," Daly declared, kneeling beside the corpse after uncovering it. Lifting up the stiff right arm with his left hand, his other fingers slid the "Green River" knife from its sheath and he went on. "I'll tell whoever's going to pay *me's* how the feller got you afore I downed him 'n' I took the gloves off 'cause they got blood all over 'em while I was doing the cutting."

Listening for sounds that would suggest somebody was approaching along the trail from either direction, the hired killer set about his grisly task with more satisfaction than distaste for what he was doing. There was no need for him to possess a knowledge of anatomy, or finesse. Manufactured from steel of an excellent quality and kept honed to a razor-sharp edge, the blade sliced into the flesh and tendons just below the heel of the hand without any difficulty. The wrist bones proved slightly more troublesome, but were quickly hacked through. Tossing down the severed hand, he wiped sweat from his face with his right sleeve. Then he set about removing the other hand. With this done, he wrapped them in the sheepskin jacket and cleaned the knife on the dead man's shirt. Sheathing the weapon, he stood up and stretched. Without bothering to cover the corpse again, he went to fasten the bundle to the cantle of the horse that had belonged to Parker.

"Good-bye, you ornery son of a bitch!" the surviving hired killer said in a mocking tone, swinging astride his mount and directing a final derisive glance at the mutilated body. "And thanks for bringing me along on this chore. It's going to pay off even better'n I figured."

8

THESE AREN'T *HIS* HANDS!

Riding in the direction from which he had come, Joel Daly left the trail to Hereford after covering about two miles and went along a much less used narrow track. Despite darkness having descended, he had experienced no difficulty in locating the rendezvous he had had described to him by Albert "Monte" Parker while riding in search of their intended victim. Wanting to locate the man who had employed his late companion and—unknowingly—himself without giving too much advance notice of his coming, he had held the two horses to a deliberately slow pace. His destination was a small line cabin showing signs of only rarely being used by the cowhands of the ranch for which it was built. Nevertheless, there was a horse tied to the hitching rail out front and he saw a faint chink of light at the edge of a piece of sack used as drapes for the window. Wishing he knew more about the arrangements that had been made for

delivering the required proof of success and obtaining
payment, he decided to act as if he were doing nothing
more than visiting by chance in case somebody with a
genuine right to be there should be inside.

"Hello the house!" the hired killer called. "Mind if I
light and rest my saddle for a spell?"

"Who's out there?" asked a muffled deep voice that
had a Midwest accent.

"Name's Monte Parker," Daly lied, believing the in-
troduction would have a meaning only for the man he
had come to meet. "I was passing and reckoned I'd stop
by for a night with a roof over my head, 'stead of sage-
henning under the stars."

"Come ahead," the speaker inside the building authorized, but without giving the slightest indication that the
name meant anything to him.

Dismounting and securing the reins of the horses to
the hitching rail, Dale studied the animal already there
as well as he could in the poor light. It was an ordinary-
looking animal, with no discernible brand to disclose its
ownership. However, the cheap range saddle carried
neither a rope nor a bedroll. Even without his voice
having indicated he was not a Texan, the former omission suggested that the rider was not a cowhand caught
at too great a distance to reach the ranch for which he
worked and was merely taking shelter for the night. On
the other hand, being without the latter implied that the
man inside had not come far and did not intend making
a lengthy journey on leaving.

Despite the conclusions he had drawn, although a
top-class *pistolero* would not have considered the precaution necessary, Daly made sure his Colt Peacemaker
was loose in its holster before going closer. Then, because of the doubts still left unsettled by the invitation,
he decided against taking the bundle inside until knowing more about the man who had spoken. He went to
the building, but as soon as he opened the door he

wished he had been more circumspect. A bull's-eye lantern on the dilapidated table in the center of the room was positioned so that it threw its beam of light straight into his eyes and, creating a dazzling effect after the darkness outside, left everything beyond it in deep shadow.

"What's *this?*" the voice demanded from the darkness, its timbre suspicious and even menacing. "You aren't Monte Parker!"

"Nope," Daly confirmed quickly, keeping his right hand well clear of the holstered Colt and raising the left to shade his eyes from the light without improving his vision to any great extent.

"I heard *two* horses coming up," the still-unseen speaker commented, his tone challenging in a way suggesting that the words were backed by a lined up and cocked gun.

"Monte took lead when we jumped the feller you sent us after," Daly explained hurriedly, guessing that he was covered and would be shot unless he was convincing.

"He didn't tell me there'd be *two* of you."

"If you knew Monte Parker, you know he was too goddamned cagey to work alone if he reckoned it'd be risky. And he wouldn't tell nobody, even the folks's hired him, anything more'n he figured they should know about the way he was fixing to do the chore. Anyways, she's been done and I've got what you asked for outside."

"Why didn't you give the signal we arranged?"

"Like I said, Monte was always a cagey son of a bitch who played his cards close to his vest. He didn't tell me nothing about no signal."

"Then who are *you?*"

"Name's Hank Smith—!"

"*Smith?*" the unseen speaker repeated, with such a chilling intonation that the hired killer felt a twinge of alarm that showed on his sallow face. "Why the hell did you pick *that* n—?" Then, because the reaction caused by the first word had been noticed, a note of mocking irony came into his voice as the question was amended. "I suppose it was just the first one to come to mind when you decided to use a *summer* name."

"Y-yeah!" Daly admitted quickly, wondering what had produced the response to the very common surname he had selected. "Like I said, Monte reckoned going after that jasper was a two-man chore and asked me to back his play. Only, he got downed afore I dropped the feller. I reckon he forgot to tell me about the signal you'd fixed up when he said where we was to come and meet you."

"From what I know of him, he more likely wasn't intending for you to stay alive long enough to be brought here and paid off," the voice said dryly, then took on a note of getting down to more important business than the possibility of Parker's treacherous intentions. "Well, have you got them?"

"They're outside," the hired killer replied, realizing that the first comment was in all probability correct and that, as Parker had been better with a gun than he was, the trap laid by the Texan could have saved his life. "I figured on find—!"

"Go and fetch them," the speaker ordered. "You got here earlier than I figured, and I don't want to stay here any longer than necessary."

Feeling uneasy, Daly turned and left the cabin without trying to complete his interrupted explanation. Having collected the bundle from the cantle of Parker's saddle, he returned. On going through the door, he found that the lantern had been moved so that its light was no longer directed into his face. However, beyond its limited range of illumination, he could still only just make out a tall and seemingly well-built shape wearing indistinct range clothes. He could not even discover whether a weapon of any kind was being held by the dark figure, but decided to continue behaving under that assumption. Stepping forward, he unrolled the coat and dumped the grisly contents onto the table.

"Here they be," the hired killer announced, hoping he looked and sounded much more confident than he was feeling. Deciding to make the explanation he had concocted before the point was raised, he went on, "The gloves got so much blood on 'em while I was doing it, I pulled 'em off 'n' threw 'em away. But here's his hands, like was asked for, and soon's I've been paid, I'll be on my way."

Even as Daly was speaking, he was struck by a belated and very alarming realization that he could have made a terrible mistake. Until that moment, he had considered the demand for the hands to be delivered as nothing more than a bizarre whim—although he would not have put the thought in those exact words—on the part of the man who wanted the Texan killed. Suddenly, he became sickeningly aware that there might be something special about them that would serve as positive identification. In that case, whatever the indications might be, Parker was unlikely to have duplicated them. As it was being arrived at, the frightening supposition received immediate verification.

"Goddamn it!" the man at the other side of the table snarled furiously. *"These* aren't *his* hands!"

Even greater alarm flooded through Daly, fueled by the appreciation of the terrible error he had made in his ignorance and the venom with which he was being addressed. Giving him no time to think of what action to take, flame lanced from the darkness and the crash of a shot from a heavy-caliber revolver resounded like a cannon in the confines of the cabin. A conical bullet spiked through his throat, rupturing flesh and blood vessels alike. Spun around by the force of the impact, he crashed face first into the wall. Choking on his own blood, he tried to turn and claw free his Colt from its holster. Before he could complete either involuntary movement, a second bullet slammed into him, this one smashing his spine. His mouth working in soundless agony, he slid down, moving slowly, almost reluctantly it seemed, until sprawling spread-eagled and dying on the floor.

Cocking his weapon, the man beyond the table gave the dying hired killer only a cursory glance. Having satisfied himself that there was nothing further to be feared from that direction, he replaced his weapon in its holster. Crossing to roll up the blankets he had spread on the floor and been using as a resting place while awaiting the arrival of Parker, he left them on the table while he went outside. On his return a short while later, he was dragging the saddles, bridles, and other items removed from the two horses brought by his victim.

"This's going to be a cheaper payoff than Parker would've got if he'd killed the son of a bitch like he was sent to do," the man declared, although he was sure the words were reaching dead ears. Picking up the roll of blankets, he hurled the lamp so it shattered against the wall and the remaining kerosene was ignited on being spilled over the dry timber. Waiting until he was sure the flames were beginning to take hold and the fire he wanted to destroy the building and its contents was well under way, he left, saying, "But it's obvious you two botched the chore and I'll have to count on those jaspers in Hereford doing better."

"Howdy, you-all," greeted the man who had escaped death in the ambush on the trail. Putting his tarpaulin-wrapped bedroll on the floor and resting the Colt rifle against the well-polished reception desk with an air of relief, he went on, "I'm not an Injun, but I reckon you should have a room on reservation for me."

"A *room*, sir?" asked the slim and bespectacled young clerk on duty at the Cattlemen's Hotel in Hereford, sounding as if he considered such levity out of place on the premises. He studied the new arrival with the calculating gaze of one desirous of ensuring that only the correct kind of people received accommodation; he had been west of the Mississippi River for long enough to draw accurate conclusions from the attire and gunbelt. Nevertheless, he glanced over his shoulder at the clock on the wall, which showed the time to be a quarter to midnight, before going on. "And what name would that be, sir?"

"Ramsbottom," the Texan supplied, glancing around the lobby as if wanting to be sure that it was deserted apart from himself and the man he was addressing.

"Ramsbottom?" the clerk could not help repeating, never having come across such a surname despite having spent all of his working life in the hotel business.

"Aloysius W. Ramsbottom the Third," the Texan elaborated with great emphasis, raising his gaze to the roof as if he had grown accustomed to and tired of such a response when introducing himself. Then, glancing at the wooden plaque on the desk, he turned a scrutiny that had become sardonic to the man behind it and continued, "It likely won't be in *my* name now I come to think on it, but *Mark Counter* will've made it. So do you have the reservation, *Mr. Barrett Wimpole Street?"*

"I'll check, sir," the clerk promised, looking at the register and, although somewhat surprised that the new-comer was aware of the connotation, silently cursing his parents—as he had many times in the past—for saddling him with such out-of-the-ordinary Christian names. As he knew was the case, there was no mention of a "Ramsbottom" on the page. Nevertheless, the information he found satisfied him that the visitor was fully acceptable as a resident regardless of the lateness of the hour. Banging the well-polished bell in front of him, he looked at the uniformed boy who came leisurely from the rear of the building and, restraining his annoyance over what he knew to be a deliberately dilatory response, ordered, "Go and tell Mr. Counter that his guest has arrived."

"Sure," the bellhop assented, turning and scuttling away with an alacrity shown only when he was sent in search of somebody he considered worthy of prompt attention.

"I don't know whether Mr. Counter has joined Mrs. Counter in their room, Mr. Ramsbottom," Street warned, adopting the tones he reserved for persons of importance. While he still had no idea who the newcomer might be, the instructions given by a man of such high standing in the cattle-raising industry suggested that a less cavalier treatment than had been accorded so far was advisable. "But he left word that he was to be called as soon as you arrived."

"That's him, Mr. Counter, sir," a boyish voice announced from the small barroom reserved for residents at the left side of the lobby before any more could be said by either man at the desk.

"*Gracias, amigo,*" replied a deep baritone voice with the drawl of a well-educated Texan. "I kind of thought it might be."

Turning, the newcomer looked at the second speaker with considerable interest.

Six feet three in height, the bareheaded man accompanying the bellhop was a magnificent physical specimen, despite having passed the first flush of youth. There was a tinge of gray to the curly golden-blond hair, but it was still luxuriant. Almost classically handsome, his tanned face had a mature strength of will and intelligence to its lines. His tremendously wide shoulders had not the slightest suggestion of sagging, although his waist had thickened out somewhat since the new arrival had last seen him. Clad in the attire of a wealthy rancher, he was not wearing a jacket. Like the white silk shirt with a neat black string bow tie, the vest and trousers—the legs hanging outside tan-colored high cow-hand-style boots—of what was obviously a three-piece brown suit were tailored to show off his build to its best advantage. However, the brown *buscadero* gunbelt, with ivory-handled Colt Cavalry Peacemakers in the contoured holsters, was designed for making a very fast draw, and he looked as if he was capable of doing so should the need arise.

"Howdy, Mr. Counter," the newcomer said, walking forward and running his right hand through the left as if seeking to straighten stiffened fingers. While doing so, he decided that the man he had come to meet did not look quite so gigantic as he had the last time their paths had crossed.[1] Darting a glance over his shoulder at the clerk, he continued, "The name's Ramsbottom, Aloysius W. Ramsbottom the Third."

"Right honored to make your acquaintance, Mr. Ramsbottom," Mark Counter asserted, showing no discernible surprise at the apparent breach of etiquette caused by the thin black leather glove not having been removed from the right hand extended his way. "Would you care to come into the bar and talk a spell, or do you want to get settled into your room first?"

"A drink'll go down real good," Ramsbottom admitted, feeling the strength of the grip he was given while shaking hands and knowing it was not being applied just to impress him. "And I could eat a bite, or seven, could it be arranged. I've been living on my own fixings for quite a spell now, which my cooking's not what it used to be—and never was."

"The dining room's closed, but the residents' bar's still open," the blond giant drawled. "And I reckon the kitchen could come up with something to eat, couldn't they, Mr. Street?"

"Of course, Mr. Counter, sir," the clerk confirmed, then his voice took on an apologetic timbre. "It will only be sandwiches, though."

"They'll do just fine, so long's the trail count tallies high," Ramsbottom declared, showing he had knowledge of the terminology of the cattle business.[2] "I wasn't expecting a full meal with all the trimmings hitting town *this* late." Turning his attention to the bellhop, he went on cheerfully, "Which livery do you have your deal with, *amigo?*"

"Deal?" the boy queried with what almost passed as wide-eyed innocence.

"Uh-huh!" the newcomer grunted, throwing a quick glance at the desk clerk and directing a knowing wink at the young youngster. "I was a bellhop myself at the Longhorn Hotel down to Los Cabestrillo when I was 'bout your age. Fact being, though I bet he don't remember me, I toted Mr. Counter's bags to his room for him one night."

"I remember being there," Mark declared with a grin. "But I don't reckon I'd've recognized you."

"Likely not," Ramsbottom admitted, also smiling. He decided against collecting the weapons belonging to his would-be killers, which were fastened to the horn of the bay's saddle, or reporting the attack to the local peace officers until he had discussed it with the blond giant. "Anyways, you'll find two mighty leg-weary hosses outside. Take them to your livery stable and have 'em 'tended to real good; they've covered plenty of long, hard miles. Tell the hosteler to keep my saddles and what's on them safe until I drop by and fetch them, *amigo.*" Pausing while he fished a silver dollar from his trousers pocket, he went on, "And, like Mr. Counter told me back when, don't spend it all on one woman."

"I don't spend *nothing* on no blasted *woman*, Mr. Ramsbottom," the youngster claimed, deftly catching the coin as it was flipped his way and wishing he could recollect a famous peace officer or gunfighter with that surname. "Which being, I'll see your hosses get 'tended *real* good 'n' your gear'll be safe no matter how long it's there. You want me to tote your bedroll and rifle up to your room first, though?"

"Be as well, I reckon," the newcomer decided. After the bellhop had collected the key for the room he had been allocated and scuttled away with his property, he turned his gaze to the blond giant. "Time was I felt that way about *women.*"

"Didn't we all?" Mark answered just as cheerfully. "You've grown a mite since that night in Los Cabestrillo."

"Now me," Ramsbottom replied, "I was just now thinking's how you'd come down in height a mite. Anyways, I bet that boy's going to be tolerable disappointed when he finds my hosses don't have the MC or OD Connected brand on them."

"Likely," the blond giant agreed, aware that his association with the second ranch was still well-known throughout the range country of Texas even though he had been running the first one mentioned for several years. "Shall we go into the bar and rest our feet?"

"You won't get no argument from *me* on that," the newcomer asserted. "Only, it's not my *feet* I want to rest right now."

1. *The meeting is described in* THE SOUTH WILL RISE AGAIN.
2. *How a "trail count" was carried out is described in* TRAIL BOSS.

9

WELCOME BACK TO TEXAS, WAXAHACHIE SMITH

"Been a long ride, huh?" Mark Counter said, more as a statement than a question, as he and his guest were crossing the lobby of the Cattlemen's Hotel.

"Long and lonesome," confirmed the man who had introduced himself to the desk clerk as Aloysius W. Ramsbottom the Third. Looking around the barroom as he entered, he discovered that he and his host had it to themselves except for the bartender. It was small, well lit, and comfortably furnished, with a second door giving access to the alley at the left side of the hotel. Having studied his surroundings in a way that implied doing so was second nature to him, he continued in the same conversational tone, "How-all's Cap'n Fog 'n' Miz Freddie?"

"Both were fit's frog's hair last time we met and're still most like' the same, seeing's how I haven't heard nothing different," Mark answered, leading the way to the table he had occupied while awaiting the arrival of his visitor. As they sat down, he went on, "They sent their respects and apologies for not being able to come and welcome you personally. In spite of your telegraph message from Santa Fe, I wasn't sure you'd get here today. But I didn't feel sleepy and reckoned I'd give you until midnight before I turned in. Anyways, how about a drink?"

"*Gracias,*" the newcomer assented. "Last time I said no to one was twenty-eight years back comes June the *thirty-second.* I'll have me a schooner of beer."

"Two schooners of beer, please, Harry, then see if you can scare up some grub for Mr. Ramsbottom here," Mark called, and while the bartender was bringing the first part of the order, he eyed his visitor with some amusement. "*Ramsbottom?*"

"I figured it'd sound more likely to be accepted by the desk clerk," the newcomer explained with a grin. "But damned if I didn't get looked at the same way I always do when I sprung it on him."

"It could be *you,* not your name, that makes folks act that way," Mark pointed out after the two schooners of beer had been brought to the table.

"Well, I'll be switched, I never thought of it like *that,*" Ramsbottom confessed. Picking up his glass, still without offering to remove the black gloves, his right forefinger continued to point straight forward. Having curled it to join the other three with his left hand, he announced, "Here's to *Texas!*"

"To Texas," the blond giant seconded, understanding the depth of genuine feeling with which the toast had been proposed. It was drunk before anything more could be said, then he went on in a tone that would not reach the bartender, who had returned to the counter. "You made good time getting here, *amigo.*"

"I figured whatever it is you want me for would be worth moving fast on," Ramsbottom claimed.

"It *will* be," Mark declared with conviction. Glancing over his shoulder and making sure the bartender had gone into the kitchen, he continued, "Welcome back to Texas, Waxa—!"

The blond giant's words were brought to an end by the sound of footsteps crossing the reception lobby to the accompaniment of the desk clerk's voice.

"Excuse me, *gentlemen!*" Barrett Wimpole Street was saying, his voice even more disapproving than it was when he had greeted the man whose name apparently was not Aloysius W. Ramsbottom the Third. "May I ask *where* you are going?"

"Where the hell do you *think?*" a harsh voice replied, and the words were slurred as if the speaker had been drinking "not wisely, but too well." He added, "In there!"

"I'm afraid you can't!" the clerk objected, his tone becoming querulous yet prohibitive. "That bar is only for residents of the hotel."

On arriving at the table they were using, which was situated in the center of the barroom, the way the two Texans had sat down would have struck anybody familiar with the habits of the West as being most significant. They had selected chairs so that their backs were not toward either the door through which they had come or the one giving access to the alley. It was, in fact, a precaution frequently adopted by men whose precarious way of life caused a need to avoid offering an opportunity for an enemy to come up behind them unseen.[1] Even without having knowledge of the thwarted ambush on the banks of the stream, an observer with range-wise eyes would see enough indications in the appearance of Ramsbottom to explain why he took it. Although less so in the case of the blond giant than was the case during his more active younger days, when seeing who was entering a room could also have meant the difference between remaining in good health and being shot in the back, he too had made his choice instinctively rather than through a desire to sit facing his visitor.

Turning their gaze toward the door through which they had entered the barroom, the blond giant and his guest studied the three men who were approaching in a loose arrowhead formation. All wore the kind of clothes that cowhands, albeit from outside Texas, had decided were most suited to the specialized needs of their work. However, there were signs that warned Mark and Ramsbottom that such was not their occupation. Nor, if the way each's right hand was going toward the butt of his low-tied revolver as they crossed the threshold, were they drunk and merely seeking to obtain further liquid refreshment in the bar reserved for residents of the Cattlemen's Hotel. If Charles Blaze had been present, he would have identified them as the attackers who escaped after the fight behind the saloon in Austin.

Lacking the information, but acting upon what he had seen and deduced while the trio were still approaching across the lobby, Ramsbottom had swiveled himself around so he was facing them and the legs of his chair were clear of the table. However, before Mark could take a similar precautionary measure, there was a distraction that caused him to direct his attention elsewhere. Somebody in the alley was trying the handle of the side door, and on finding it locked, let out an explosive profanity. Then there was a crash as the glass pane in it, the bottom half painted white and the top bearing the words "CATTLEMEN'S HOTEL, Residents Only" to further restrict vision beyond, was burst asunder by the butt of the sawed-off shotgun held by the taller of two men outside. Even if his weapon had not served as sufficient indication, the Colt being wielded by his companion removed any slight chance that they were merely residents acting in anger on finding they could not gain admittance by conventional means.

Instead of looking around, Ramsbottom kept his at-

tention on the trio at the connecting door, leaving the
blond giant to cope with whatever might be happening
in the direction of the commotion. Making the most of
an advantage offered by the rig he was wearing, he had
no need to leave his seat before he started to arm himself in the fashion required by the way he carried his
Colt Civilian Model Peacemaker. Turning his right elbow outward and almost to shoulder level, thankful that
the chair did not have armrests to impede him, he ro-
tated his hand swiftly so that it closed upon the inner
side of the staghorn grip. Not unexpectedly, as they had
been carried out to convert it into what was known as a
"slip gun,"[2] the modifications that had helped bring
about the downfall of Monte Parker failed to cause him
similar problems. His forefinger passed through the
empty trigger guard, but did not alter its curvature to
press against the back when inside. Clamping his second
and third fingers firmly on the butt, he hooked the
fourth under the base to grant an increased support.
While this was taking place, his thumb was coiling over
the shortened, lowered, and smoothed spur of the hammer. Then, by snapping his elbow inward, he not only
twisted the revolver from the form-fitting Missouri Skin-
Tite holster but cocked the single action without needing further effort from the thumb.

Although he had led a much less eventful life recently, Mark proved he had lost little of the speed that
frequently served to keep him alive in similarly dangerous situations while he was riding with Dusty Fog as a
member of the OD Connected ranch's floating outfit.[3]
However, carrying his Colt Cavalry Model Peacemakers
in the more conventional fashion, he realized he could
not draw them as effectively as his companion was doing
while sitting down. Nor did he attempt to do so. Instead,
sending his chair skidding away with a thrust from his
thighs, he grasped the edge of the table in both hands as
he came erect like a startled cock pheasant leaving

cover. Showing he still possessed much of the strength for which he had been famous in his younger days, he swung the table upward. It passed over Ramsbottom's head without impeding the smooth flow of the special "slip gun" draw.

Three-quarters of a second from the first movement, having pointed the Colt at waist level instinctively while the table was going over him, Ramsbottom relaxed the grip his thumb was applying. Freed from restraint, the hammer snapped forward to plunge its striker into the priming cap of the cartridge in the cylinder's uppermost chamber. The crash of exploding black powder sounded and, indicative of the skill with which the weapon was being handled, the leader of the trio was struck in the chest. There had been only one shot, but three holes appeared in his shirt. However, although the apertures were smaller than would have been the case if a single .45-caliber bullet had arrived, he was slammed backward before he could fire a shot.

As soon as the table was sent on its way, Mark's hands lashed downward to enfold the ivory grips of his revolvers. Their seven-and-a-half-inch barrels were swept from the carefully designed holsters with only slightly less rapidity than he could produce in his hectic youth. However, they did not speak straightaway. While the impromptu missile prevented the taller man from being able to bring the sawed-off shotgun into alignment, or the other from using the revolver, it also shielded them from the blond giant's view. Nevertheless, when it crashed into the door and fell to the floor, he was ready. The Colts thundered almost in unison and sent their bullets with an equal accuracy. Selected as posing the greater possible threat, the man with the shotgun was taken in the chest by both pieces of lead and hurled backward across the alley.

Swiftly though Ramsbottom had dealt with the first of the trio, his instincts as an exceptionally competent gunfighter warned that he and his host were still in considerable danger. The other two from the lobby were unharmed and showed no signs of being put off by the original stages of what had the makings of a well-conceived plan going badly wrong. While he believed he would be able to take care of one, the distance they were apart removed any possibility of being able to turn and use the slip gun quickly enough to prevent the other from firing at him. What was more, he could expect no assistance from the blond giant, who was fully occupied with what Ramsbottom realized must be more attackers at the other side of the room.

Having taken care of the man with the shotgun, Mark gave his attention immediately to the second would-be assailant. He was granted the vitally necessary pause because this one's view was partially blocked until the window was broken, and because the other's body was an obstruction before it was thrown backward under the impact of the two .45-caliber bullets. Brief though the respite was, it proved sufficient for the man who in his heyday was reputed to be second only to the legendary Rio Hondo gun wizard, Dusty Fog, in the speed and accuracy with which he could use a brace of Colts.[4] On this occasion, instead of firing simultaneously with both guns, he started to thumb back each hammer in turn. Then, squeezing the appropriate trigger and riding the not-inconsiderable recoils with the aid of long training and his exceptional strength, he discharged shot after shot in a continuous drumroll of explosions.

Electing to take the man on the right side, having deduced he was the more capable of the pair, Ramsbottom responded with the same devastating speed that had characterized his handling of the modified Colt. Nevertheless, even as the triple ball load was being dispatched and found its marks as effectively as had its predecessor, he knew he would be too late to save himself from the other. Already the revolver held by the surviving member of the trio was being pointed at him, and he felt sure its user possessed the ability to ensure it made a hit.

Gushing from the twin muzzles in turn, the white smoke from the detonated powder in eight cartridge cases swirled thickly before the blond giant. However, this proved to be a mixed blessing. While it served to make him a more obscure target, the same applied to the man at whom he was firing. Nevertheless, continuing to send the bullets in the general direction of the shattered pane in the door, he achieved his purpose.

Reaching the window, the second attacker found himself in the middle of a veritable hail of flying lead. None of it touched him, but one bullet tore the hat from his head and he felt the wind, or heard the eerie *splat!* sound as others went by very close. He failed in his attempt to count how many times the long-barreled Colts had spoken, the speed of the discharges having rendered this impossible. On the other hand, he could see enough to realize that the rest of his companions were not meeting with success against the second Texan. Deciding that the ambush had failed, he turned to race along the alley without offering to try to retrieve his headgear, and the pattering of his departing footsteps quickly faded away.

Despite having removed the peril from that side, Mark could not have turned and used the single remaining bullet in either Colt quickly enough to offer assistance to his guest.

Salvation came from another and most unexpected source.

For all his pompous and prissy manner when on duty, Barrett Wimpole Street was neither a fool nor lacking in courage. What was more, he possessed a strong sense of loyalty to his employers and was all too aware of the responsibilities that went with his positions of desk clerk and night manager. Annoyed by the way his warning

about the status of the residents' barroom was ignored
by the newcomers, who he had assumed were nothing
more than drunken cowhands, hearing the shooting
gave notice of his error in judgment. While he was startled by the unexpected turn of events, such a thing never
having happened at the Cattlemen's Hotel—or anywhere else he had served in a similar capacity—he was
not frozen into frightened immobility.

On the shelf under the desk, kept loaded and available for use in such an emergency, was a Smith & Wesson .38-caliber double-action revolver. Unlikely as such
a thing might have struck most people who came into
contact with him during working hours, Street had acquired enough competence in its use to expect that it
would allow him to protect the clientele of the hotel.
Despite having heard of Mark Counter's ability as a
gunfighter and seeing the first man shot by Ramsbottom
reeling backward through the door, he snatched up the
weapon with his right hand and, raising it to shoulder
height as he was taught, adopted the stance he had
found gave the best results when firing at a target.

"Stop that, or I'll *fire!*" the clerk yelled, standing sideways to the door and lining up the revolver as the second of Ramsbottom's victims blundered into view after
the first.

Anybody possessing a greater knowledge of such matters could have warned Street that his behavior was ill-
advised and could put his own life in danger. However,
in one respect, the clerk might have counted himself
fortunate. Being alerted to the threat he was posing, the
surviving man—to whom the words were directed—
might have turned and reacted in a manner he would be
unable to counter. While he was a good shot, he had
never fired at another human being, or, in fact, on a
living target of any kind. Nor was he aware of just how
swiftly a skilled gunfighter could respond to the situation he had created.

The last of the would-be attackers was unable to prevent himself from glancing around on hearing Street, but he was not allowed to take any action against the possible threat from that direction. While part of his mind absorbed the potential danger from the lobby, the rest was just as cognizant of the greater peril in the barroom. However, he failed to stop an involuntary wavering of his Colt from its original target.

Small though the movement was, it proved sufficient for a man with Ramsbottom's capabilities. Swinging swiftly, almost as if of its own volition and drawn by some magnetic force, the slip gun changed its point of aim. Appreciating the danger Street had brought upon himself by shouting, its owner began to operate the hammer and fire with all the speed he could muster. Three times the specialized weapon crashed, at a pace only "fanning" could achieve with a single-action revolver that had not been modified in such a fashion. Yet, despite the rapidity, the barrel was moved slightly between each detonation and the nine components of the multi-ball loads spread as if sent through a shotgun. Four of them missed, but the rest found their way into the body of the man before he could rectify his error and return his Colt to its original alignment. Letting out an abbreviated profanity as the pieces of lead tore into his body, he twirled on his heels. As he was colliding against the wall, the weapon slipping from his grasp, he measured his length on the floor.

"Are you all right, Mark?" Ramsbottom inquired, satisfied that he had ended his part of the threat.

"Why, sure," the blond giant replied, turning around without holstering his guns even though he, too, considered the danger to be over. "And, like I was saying just before we were interrupted, welcome back to Texas, Waxahachie Smith."

"*Gracias,*" Ramsbottom replied, making no protest over the name by which he had been addressed. "Only, seeing's how this's the *second* time I've had to stop jaspers trying to kill me since I crossed the New Mexico line, I'm beginning to wonder how come *somebody* doesn't want sweet, lovable, li'l ole me to come back."

1. *The tragic results of James Butler "Wild Bill" Hickok failing for once to take the precaution of sitting where he could not be approached from behind are described in* Part Seven, "Deadwood, August the 2nd, 1876," J. T.'s HUNDREDTH.
2. *How and why the modifications to the staghorn-handled Colt Civilian Model Peacemaker revolver were carried out is told in* NO FINGER ON THE TRIGGER.
3. *Information about Mark Counter's family background, career, and special qualifications can be found in the Appendix.*
4. *An occasion when Mark Counter proved himself second only to Dusty Fog in speed on the draw and accurate shooting is recorded in* GUN WIZARD.

10

I RECKON YOU'VE MADE
SOME ENEMIES

"The *second* time?" Mark Counter repeated, a frown creasing his almost classically handsome features.

While speaking, returning the left-hand Colt Cavalry Peacemaker to its contoured holster, the blond giant opened the loading gate on the right side at the rear end of the other revolver's six-capacity cylinder. Using the spring-operated ejector rod beneath the seven-and-a-half-inch-long barrel to remove each empty case in turn from the chambers, he replaced it with a live round drawn out of the loops on his *buscadero* gunbelt. Such was the skill he had attained over the years, he did not need to look down at what he was doing and instead glanced through the connecting door between the bar-room and the entrance lobby. Looking pale and shaken by what had happened, Barrett Wimpole Street was coming from behind the desk with the Smith & Wesson revolver dangling by his side. What was more, he was only the first of those wanting to investigate the commotion. Several of the guests from the other two floors were appearing on the stairs.

"Why, sure," Waldo "Waxahachie" Smith confirmed, starting to replenish the slip gun with an equal facility. "This's the *second* time today somebody's tried to shoot me down."

"Whee dogie!" Mark exclaimed, then contrived to give a shrug without halting the reloading. "And to think's how we picked on here to meet you because we figured it'd be *safe!*"

"Which being, I'm right pleased you didn't pick on some place's might've proved *dangerous,*" the reddish-haired Texan commented dryly, wondering whether he would be expected to carry on employing the alias Aloysius W. Ramsbottom the Third when the local peace officers arrived. Before he could raise the point, he saw the desk clerk approaching and his voice lost the bantering timbre it had held on his arrival as he turned in that direction. "Like to thank you for shouting the way you did, Mr. Street. 'Though there's a few folks here and there's might say I'm not worth it, you saved my life."

"I'm pleased to have been of service, Mr. Ramsbottom" the desk clerk answered. Having looked from one to the other of the bodies sprawled on the lobby's floor in passing and put the Smith & Wesson in his jacket's pocket, he had swung his gaze around on entering the barroom. "Such a thing has *never—!*"

"Maybe you'd best keep everybody out of here until the sheriff comes," Mark suggested gently, seeing an expression of nausea creeping across Street's face and bringing the explanation to an end uncompleted.

"I—I will!" the clerk accepted, struggling to keep control over his stomach as it sought to expel the supper he had eaten and returning to the lobby hurriedly, but avoiding even another glance at the corpses.

"I'll be damned if that li'l feller wasn't ready to take on these jaspers to protect *us,*" Smith drawled with admiration. "He's more of a man than I reckoned when we first met, and I'd be wolf bait for sure now if he hadn't yelled to make the third of 'em turn away just long enough for me to cut loose."

"I'm right pleased he did," Mark drawled, glancing through the door to where the first of the guests were approaching.

"That makes two of us," Smith asserted with a wry grin. "And *me* more than you, likely. I'm all I've got."

"There's some might say you deserve pitying for *that,*" the blond giant drawled, also smiling. "Only, I won't tell you where I stand on it."

Despite his queasy stomach, Street proved capable of carrying out the instructions from Mark. However, although he stopped the rest with a firmness that was far different from his normal demeanor when dealing with the influential people who used the Cattlemen's Hotel, he allowed one person to pass.

The exception was a tall and slender woman a few years younger than Mark, an ankle-length blue silk robe wrapped tightly around her and Comanche moccasins on her feet. There was just a hint of silvery gray in her blond hair, which had been taken back in a tight bun suitable for wearing to bed, and she had a good-looking, tanned face imbued with lines of maturity and character. She did no more than direct a quick look with no discernible emotion at the three bodies in passing, but showed concern as she hurried into the barroom. However, it faded when she saw the blond giant standing uninjured and placing the now reloaded Peacemaker by its mate.

"There's been a mite of trouble, honey," Mark said, commencing the replenishment of the second revolver.

"I kind of got the notion there might have been," the

woman replied with the accent of a Texan. "What started it?"

"We don't know yet," the blond giant admitted. "Could be they were after Mr. Ramsbottom here."

"Mr. Ramsbottom?" the woman queried, eyeing Smith in a speculative fashion.

"Aloysius W. Ramsbottom, the *Third*," Mark elaborated loudly enough to be heard by Street and the onlookers. Then, lowering his voice, he went on, "Wax, meet my wife. Dawn, this here's Waxahachie Smith."[1]

"Hello, Wax," the woman greeted, speaking no louder.

"Howdy, Miz Counter, ma'am," Smith replied, thrusting the Colt slip gun—its cylinder once again charged with multi-ball cartridges—back into the Missouri Skin-Tite holster. However, although he swept off his hat with a courtly gesture indicative of good manners, he did not make another change of raiment dictated by convention before offering to accept the right hand held his way. "Hoping you'll excuse the gloves, ma'am, but—"

"I understand," Dawn said gently and sympathetically. Then, knowing the reason for the omission and sensing that the subject was a particularly delicate one to the man she was addressing, she went on, "Where on earth did you dig up Aloysius W. Ramsbottom, the Third? It's one hell of a high-toned summer name."

"I picked it out *real* careful, ma'am," the reddish-haired Texan replied, speaking so soberly he might have been imparting information of the greatest importance and expecting it to be noted. "See, I reckoned with something that fancy, folks'd be more likely to take kindly to me than if I let on I was just a plain ole Smith."

"And have they?" Dawn queried with a smile.

"Not if those yahoos are anything to go on," Smith admitted, gesturing to the lobby. "Or the other two."

"Which other two?" Dawn asked, looking to her husband and then back at the other Texan.

"You'll hear all about it when Tom Maskell gets here, honey," Mark answered.

"Which's right now," Smith stated, nodding to where two new arrivals were coming through the front entrance to the lobby. Showing a family resemblance, they were dressed in Texas-style range clothes. Each had the badge of a peace officer on his vest and supplemented his low-tied Colt Peacemaker with a short-barreled shotgun. "Happen Tom Maskell's the sheriff."

"He's sheriff, which's how come we picked here to meet you," Mark confirmed, and put away the second revolver. "Howdy, Tom, Wilf."

"Howdy, Dawn, Mark," the shorter and older of the local peace officers responded as both took off their hats in deference to the presence of a lady. However, although he was not being spoken to, they were giving Smith the majority of their attention. "Looks like you've been having more than a mite of trouble."

"You could say that," the blond giant drawled before his guest could speak. "But give credit where it's due, we managed to have it *afore* you went off watch. There's some who'd've waited until you gone home and got to bed."

"Why, thank you 'most to death for being so thoughtful," Sheriff Thomas Maskell said dryly. In his mid-forties, he was leathery faced and had the bearing of an outdoorsman. Neat and clean, his attire was not so expensive as to raise suspicions with regard to his means of purchasing it. All in all, even without having heard of his reputation, he would have struck Smith as being honest and competent. "Was *you* in on this, Mr.—?"

"*Ramsbottom*," Mark introduced. "Aloysius W. Ramsbottom the Third. He's the gent I wrote and told you we'd be meeting up with here."

"Howdy, Mr.—*Ramsbottom*," the sheriff greeted, his

gaze going to the black gloves still worn by the man he was addressing.

"Howdy, Sheriff," the reddish-haired Texan replied, then his voice took on a complaining timbre. "Way folks always say my name comes summer, I almost wish I'd been born plain ole Smith."

"You'd likely have a tolerable slew of kinfolks here and thereabouts if it was," the lanky deputy sheriff commented amiably, sharing his superior's satisfaction over the way they had been informed that Ramsbottom was only a summer name. "Might even be some of 'em down to Waxahachie."

"Wouldn't surprise me none at all," Smith admitted, although his parents were dead and no other members of his family had been living in the town that was his birthplace when he had left. "But there're no Ramsbottoms there."

"I'll bet the good folks of Waxahachie figure *that's* a crying shame," the sheriff declared sardonically. Then he glanced at the shattered window in the side door and went on, "Was them three in the lobby all of 'em?"

"You'll find another out there, likely dead seeing's how there wasn't time to try nothing fancy like just nicking him," Mark replied. "Had an *amigo,* but he lit a shuck like he'd got real important business elsewhere and's likely long gone."

"Go take a look, Cousin Wilf," Maskell instructed. "Then you'd best help 'Rett Street send all those good folks back to their rooms and pass the word for Jones the Burial to come and move the bodies to his place. The lights were still on's we came by, so he'll likely be headed here looking for business."

"You surely like to give the good taxpaying folks hereabouts plenty of value for my pay," claimed Deputy Sheriff Wilfred Piggot, who looked like a younger, slightly taller version of his uncle and had already acquired a similar reputation for honesty. Glancing to where the local undertaker was crossing the lobby followed by two Chinamen clad in an equally somber fashion, he continued, "Do you reckon they'll feel cheated 'cause he's got here, 'stead of me having to go fetch him?"

"Likely not," the sheriff assessed dryly. "Howdy, *Mr*. Jones. Sorry you had to turn out this late."

"That's all right," the black-clad newcomer replied, his voice tinged with the singsong lilt common to the country of his origins. Although not on terms of friendship with the peace officer—as was indicated by the emphasis on the honorific and employment of his surname—he had once explained that he had acquired his sobriquet because his family had been undertakers for generations and Jones was such a common surname in the Welsh valley from which his family had emigrated that some form of definition was necessary to differentiate among them. "I was just finishing off that Box L cowhand ready for burial tomorrow, so I thought I would come to see if there was any work for me."

"Bueno, 'cause there is," Maskell said. "Can you handle things if Cousin Wilf lends a hand?"

"There isn't any need for him to do that, look you," Llewellyn Jones asserted. "I've my own men here, and you might need him."

"We'll leave it's you're Aloysius W. Ramsbottom the Third, for the time being," the sheriff declared after the undertaker had walked away and he was seated with the Counters and Smith at a table in the center of the barroom. He held his voice to a level that would not reach the ears of anybody in the lobby. "So let's start by you telling me what happened."

"And, way things turned out," Mark claimed at the conclusion of his and Smith's explanations, "there wasn't anything else we could do."

"You won't get any argument from me on *that,*" Maskell promised.

"But you will from *me,*" Dawn stated, eyeing her husband grimly. "You're getting too old for this sort of thing, Mark Counter."

"I'll try to keep it in mind, honey," the blond giant promised, laying a big hand on and gently shaking his wife's head a couple of times. " 'Cepting I don't recollect *ever* being young enough to reckon this sort of thing was a sociable and fun-filled way of spending an evening."

"I didn't see any of those three in the lobby about town while I was making the rounds earlier," the sheriff remarked. "So they must've just rode in. Leastwise, there're three hosses loose tied to the hitching rail outside that'll likely belong to them. Do you reckon they were the bunch who were hanging around your spread, Mark?"

"Somebody was after *you?*" Smith inquired of the blond giant.

"They didn't try anything, if they was," Mark replied. "A couple of our hands were riding the home range and came in to say they'd seen signs like five or six fellers were watching the trail. I got me some more of the crew and we went to take a look, but they either saw us coming and lit a shuck, or they just happened to be passing through. As luck would have it, we'd a bunch of mares to fetch up and put to stud with Tolly Maxwell's stallion. So to be on the safe side, Dawn and I came with the boys who're delivering them. There was some dust rising over a rim behind us 'bout halfway, but we didn't see who, or what, was stirring it."

"Which don't help us decide who-all this bunch was after," Maskell complained wryly and looked at the reddish-haired Texan. "Didn't you say something about this being the *second* time somebody'd tried to jump you tonight?"

"Why, sure," Smith confirmed. " 'Cepting the first

time was earlier today, out along the trail near the New Mexico line."

"Whereabouts along the trail?" Maskell inquired with what appeared to be a hopeful air. "Was it in Texas or *their* side of the line?"

"In Texas, I reckon," Smith supplied.

"It *would* be," the sheriff said, realizing that the location must be within the boundaries of Deaf Smith County. Although it did not fool his audience, there seemed to be bitter resignation in his tone as he went on. "Where'd it happen?"

"I'd just crossed a stream when they tried to jump me," Smith explained. "But I didn't see nothing to tell me its name, if it's got one."

"That'll be Palo Duro Creek," the sheriff assessed. "Which being, it *is* in Texas and on my bailiwick, blast the luck. So it falls on poor ole me to go look things over in the morning. Until then, did you know them?"

"Never seen either of 'em afore, as far as I can recollect."

"And this bunch tonight?"

"Can't bring to mind ever having crossed trails with the three in the lobby."

"How about the two in the alley?"

"I didn't see either of them," Smith admitted.

"Take a look afore the undertaker gets out there," the sheriff suggested.

"He's as much of a stranger as the rest of 'em," Smith assessed, having gone with the blond giant and Maskell to the door giving access to the alley and looked through the shattered pane. "But, like I said, I didn't see the other jasper. What'd he look like, Mark?"

"I didn't get too good a look at him myself," the blond giant confessed, and gave what few details he had observed while returning to the table.

"That doesn't ring no bells, neither," Smith claimed. "Until those three jumped me in here, I thought the first pair were just owlhoots figuring on bushwhacking me for what I'm toting. Not out of anything *personal*, but just 'cause it happened to be *me* coming along. I'm sort of lucky that way."

"No offense, mind, Wa—*Mr. Ramsbottom*," Maskell said. "But I reckon you've made *some* enemies in your time?"

"Surprising's it might seem, me being so pleasant-natured 'n' all, I've not left everybody feeling best pleased with me here and there," Smith answered. "Only, I can't bring to mind anybody who'd be riled up enough to hire so many guns to be hunting for my scalp."

"How about the kin of those Fuentes brothers you had fuss with down to Bonham County while you was with the Rangers?" the sheriff inquired, and glanced pointedly at the reddish-haired Texan's hands. "Being high-born Mexicans, what happened 'tween you and their late kin, they'd likely figure the family's honor called for 'em to look for evens against you."

"They sent a couple of *hombres* gunning for me not long after I'd made wolf bait of Teodoro and that drug-crazed brother of his," Smith replied, also looking at the black gloves in which only the thumb, second, third, and fourth fingers on each side moved restlessly. "But neither went back and no more's come. Or, happen they were sent, they made good and sure's they didn't find me. Anyways, the Fuentes family wouldn't—or *shouldn't*—know's I was headed here. Which, should it be me and not Mark, these fellers had to have done *both* times."

"We've *tried* to keep asking you to come back and where we'd meet up with you a secret, Wax," Mark stated, aware there was a good reason for such a precaution to be taken. "But, like we all know, even what should've been the best-kept secrets have a nasty habit of getting out."

"With what's at stake," Maskell commented, "I'd've

thought *everybody* would want it done bad enough not to care who was helping to do it."

"Not everybody wants it done, Tom," Dawn pointed out. "And those who don't will be real eager to do anything they can to stop it."

"You're right, honey, like always," Mark supported. "And it looks like they've already made a start at trying said stopping. Which being, we'll have to make a stab at finding out who-all *doesn't* want it to happen bad enough to pull a game like this to spoil it—and stop them all the way up to the Green River."

1. *How and where Mark Counter met his wife, Dawn—her maiden name being Sutherland—is told in* GOODNIGHT'S DREAM *and* FROM HIDE AND HORN.
2. *Told in* NO FINGER ON THE TRIGGER.

11

HAVE YOU EVER HEARD OF THE "TEXAS FEVER"?

"Howdy, Mr. Ramsbottom," Dawn Counter greeted as Waxahachie Smith came over to the table in the dining room where she and her husband were having a belated breakfast at half past eleven in the morning. "Won't you join us?"

Despite the events of the previous evening and the lateness of her finally being able to retire to bed, Dawn looked calm and fully rested. She had on a tailored costume for women that was almost masculine in style, a white shirt-blouse with collar and cuffs, and a man's dark blue silk bow tie. Indicative of the fact that she still spent considerable time on horseback when on the MC ranch, the sharp toes of black cowhand riding boots showed from beneath the hem of the long and flared skirt.

"Well, thank you kindly, ma'am," Smith accepted, sitting down. While approaching, he had not been unduly surprised to discover that everybody else was looking his way. Like Mark, except for having put on a clean shirt, he was dressed in the same fashion as on the previous evening and had on his gunbelt. However, he knew it was his participation in the gunfight that was causing the interest being shown in him. "I reckon I just about *could* eat a mite, or even two mites, was I pressed on it, seeing's how I didn't get any supper last night, what with one thing and another."

"That was unfortunate," Dawn sympathized. "Anyway, after all the fuss, did you have a good night, *Mr. Ramsbottom?*"

"Why, sure, ma'am," Smith drawled, again noticing the slight emphasis placed on his summer name. "Leastwise, I got through it without anybody else trying to gun me down. Not even *once.*"

"You sound disappointed," Dawn commented. "Perhaps somebody will oblige you before you've finished eating."

"A man can only hope," Smith claimed, also speaking as soberly as if the exchange of remarks were serious. Looking up at the waitress who had come over, he stated, "I'll have some waffles in syrup, ma'am, a couple of eggs fried sunny-side up, and maybe a few rashers of bacon—only, not *too* few."

"Very good, sir," the woman replied.

Despite Smith's having been consumed by curiosity the previous night, it had not been satisfied beyond what he had already heard while the local peace officers were conducting their investigation. The shooting had aroused much interest among the hotel's residents, and several of the men had declined to follow the instructions to return to their respective rooms relayed from Sheriff Thomas Maskell by Deputy Sheriff Wilfred Piggot. Half a dozen of them remained in the entrance lobby during the interview with the two Texans, and the departure of the peace officers had presented the op-

portunity they were seeking. They had entered the barroom to get drinks and ask questions, which prevented
the Counters and Smith from being able to continue the
discussion. What was more, all the men were of such
importance in various ways that Mark had intimated to
Smith it would be impolitic to refuse to speak to them.
Not being dressed suitably for masculine company and
because the barroom was regarded as being no place for
a "good" woman under normal conditions, Dawn had
let her husband and their guest to do the talking.

On Smith's being introduced by Mark, most of the
men who had gathered at the counter were sufficiently
knowledgeable of Western matters to realize that he
was not merely a chance passing cowhand. However,
none had given any hint of suspecting that Al Ramsbottom—which the blond giant had considered more
suitable to the occasion than employing the full summer
name—was an alias. Instead of either participant dis-
closing the earlier ambush to which Smith was subjected, or their suppositions with regard to its possible
connection to the latest incident, they gave the impression that they believed the latter to be nothing more
than an attempt to rob the hotel. Although this appeared to have been accepted by their audience, the
bartender was kept too busy serving drinks to provide
the sandwiches promised on the arrival of the reddish-
haired Texan, and he had gone to bed hungry.

"Despite what's happened since you got into Texas,
Al," Mark commented as the waitress walked away and,
without making his scrutiny obvious, he glanced around
the room as if wishing to make sure nobody was near
enough to listen, "I reckon you'll be interested in hearing why you've been asked to come back?"

"That's more of *'specially* than *despite,* if you don't
mind me saying so," Smith corrected. "Things've happened's makes even a slow-thinking li'l ole country boy

like me reckon he might not be's welcome hereabouts as his pleasant nature calls for."

"The first thing, Al," the blond giant said in an apologetic tone, "is that things've had to stay as they are with you and the law in Texas."

"Dusty, Freddie, and Mark are doing everything they can to get the governor to change his mind, Al," Dawn stated.

"I didn't need to be told *that*, ma'am," Smith asserted, despite having hoped the political advisability of making him a wanted man and liable for arrest if he returned to his home state had been ended. "You've all done everything you could for me right from the beginning."

"And we're *still* doing it," Mark claimed. "But every time we try to have it brought before the state legislature, those goddamned liber-rad softshells in the capital start howling how Texas'll be breaking faith with the Mexican government should you be given a pardon without a real good reason. What's more, they get backing from their kind in Washington, D.C., which tends to make the governor—or at least his advisers—more than a mite reluctant to do it."

"Politicians!" Smith grunted, making the word sound obscene.

"Like Miz Freddie says real frequent, like the poor, they're always with us and we're stuck with 'em," the blond giant drawled philosophically. "But there's *one* good thing about politicians—at least, the kind who count where you're concerned. If you pull off what we've asked you to come back for, there isn't any way on God's good earth those knobheads in Austin'll dare hold back on giving you a pardon."

"It's that important, huh?" the reddish-haired Texan inquired.

"It's just about the most important thing to happen to Texas since Colonel Goodnight showed how we could make plenty of money taking trail herds to places that paid better than the hide-and-tallow factories were doing just after the War," Mark estimated somberly.[1] "And in spite of this crude old black oil stuff's keeps cropping up and some folks have such high hopes on, the cattle business is still way out the biggest earner for the state."

"And something's threatening the cattle business?" Smith assessed, more as a statement than a question.

"You've never been righter," the blond giant confirmed. "Have you ever heard of the Texas fever out where you've been?"

"Why, sure," Smith admitted. "Not much, though. Which being, something tells me I'm going to need to know a whole heap more than I do now afore I'm through with this chore—or even started on it, comes to that."

"You'll know what *we* know," Mark promised. "Only, that isn't much."

"I don't think Al will need to know more than we do, honey," Dawn commented.

"Likely not," Mark acceded. "Anyways, Al, it's a disease that's been spreading in the Indian Nations and Kansas, mostly along the trails that herds from down here in Texas've used to get to the railroad. Wasn't noticed too much in the early days, likely because there wasn't a whole heap of folks living there and them who did weren't handling much livestock. Well, likely you know how folks've been closer to flooding in than just moving west over the last few years—?"

"I've seen some of it, even as far west's I've been spending most of my time just recent'," Smith admitted. "Can't say I'm for it. Trouble being, now it's started and there's all those folks being talked into coming over from Europe's'll be needing land to settle on, I don't reckon there's any way of stopping it."

"There's one thing about all those said folks that

hasn't gone unnoticed by politicians wherever they go and in Washington, D.C.," Mark declared. "Sooner or later, 'most all of them'll be able to vote comes election time. Which being, their wantings've got to be watched out for. And one of the things they want in the Nations and Kansas is to stop the Texas fever spreading around their livestock."

"Nobody can blame them for wanting *that*," the reddish-haired Texan stated.

"Nor do any of us cattlemen down here to Texas," the blond giant asserted. "What's worrying us is the way it keeps getting suggested the said stopping should be done."

"That wouldn't be by saying 'You gents from Texas can't bring no more cattle over our land,' now would it?"

"It's getting talked about more and more up North. You know how the softshells's hate *everybody* to do with the South, 'less'n it's black folks who can be patronized into believing they're all for 'em and'll give them their votes. So you'll not be oversurprised to hear they've got *their* newspapers printing the notion more than anybody else."

"How close are they to getting the trail herds stopped?"

"They haven't got anywhere *legally* as yet," Mark replied. "But there's talk they're spreading about what they call 'honest and upright citizens' being driven to form a 'Winchester quarantine' to protect their livestock from the 'dreadful Texas fever.' You know the kind of things they write and say?"

"I've read 'em on the 'rights' of thieves and murderers not to be treated mean or interfered with by peace officers," Smith claimed, his tone showing how he regarded such articles in the liberal-radical newspapers. He could also see how the armed intervention, which he felt sure the suggestions were deliberately trying to provoke, would create an explosive situation wherever it was met by the Texans handling the trail herds. "So I can imagine what they're saying. Anyways, how do I come into it?"

"Freddie and Dusty know a feller who reckons he can find the cure, but needs to come to where he can do some experimenting with cattle afore they're moved north," Mark explained. Giving no indication of noticing how the reddish-haired Texan was behaving, he continued, "So we want *you* to go collect him from where they met, bring him down to Texas, and stay by him while he's working on it."

While the conversation was taking place, Smith had become increasingly aware of the sensation that always arose when he was under observation beyond merely a passing glance. It was a trait developed and honed fine over several years, first as a Texas Ranger and then as a roaming professional gunfighter of the legitimate kind, when trouble had been his regular bedfellow. Acting in response to it had saved his life on more than one occasion. Therefore, always willing to accept its warning, he had begun to glance around surreptitiously with the intention of discovering who was looking him over and estimate whether any threat was posed by the scrutiny.

Although there were a few of the men whom Smith had met the previous night in the residents' barroom, none were seated close by, apparently having accepted that the Counters did not wish for company. Nor were the only two strangers present. However, because he had not already made their acquaintance, he gave them a close and surreptitious examination.

Despite its seeming unlikely that he could have been conducting the scrutiny, the bigger of the pair attracted most of Smith's attention. Seated so his back was almost turned toward the Texans, he was tall and well built and had on the attire of a successful professional gambler. However, instead of being fitted with the cross-draw rig

frequently selected as better suited to the purpose of
one who would be most likely to need it while sitting at
a table in a game of chance, his well-designed gunbelt
carried its ivory-handled Colt Civilian Model Peacemaker in a low-hanging fast-draw holster. The few
glimpses he gave of his face established that it was hard
and had a tan that seemed to indicate far more time
spent outdoors than under a roof engaged in the occupation for which he was dressed.

Compared with his companion, the second man was
less noticeable and, in fact, almost undistinguished in
appearance. In fact, even though he was facing forward
and could have been conducting the observation, Smith
would not have given him a second glance except for the
company he was keeping. Tallish and slender in build,
with a mane of white hair and an enormous drooping
mustache that was his most prominent aspect, he appeared to be past the prime of life. His pallid face was
lined and wrinkled, with nothing except for its hirsute
adornment to set it apart. Not only was the brown three-
piece Eastern suit he had on clearly inexpensive, it fitted
badly and was of a style long passed from fashion. There
was no sign of his being armed. Certainly he was not
wearing a gunbelt. When he was addressed by the gambler, he leaned forward as if hard of hearing.

Before Smith could draw any conclusions about the
pair as the source of his disturbed feeling, or the problems arising from the Texas fever could be discussed
further, the arrival of Sheriff Maskell caused considerations of both issues to be postponed. Although nothing
showed on his leathery face, there were enough indications in the rest of his demeanor for the Counters and
Smith to guess he was bringing news of importance.

"I ate at a respectable hour, not like *some* folks I
might mention," the peace officer declared with mock
unctuous virtue when Dawn invited him to join them for
breakfast. "But I reckon a cup of Arbuckle's won't come

amiss, no matter whether it's the genuine article or not."

"There're *some* who might say you don't deserve one after what you just said," Dawn asserted, exuding an equally spurious severity, but she poured some of the steaming black liquid from the coffeepot into an unused cup. "And what might you have been doing since that respectable hour?"

"Wilf and me rode out to Palo Duro Creek to take a look at that jasper you had to shoot, Wa—*Mr. Ramsbottom,*" Maskell explained. "Thought it'd be quicker than waiting for Jones the Burial's hearse to fetch him in."

"Wasn't he there?" the reddish-haired Texan asked, deducing that something out of the ordinary had been discovered by the peace officers on their arrival at the scene of the abortive ambush.

"Oh sure, he was there all right," the sheriff replied, but with reservations. "Most of him, anyways."

"*Most* of him?" Dawn queried when neither Mark nor Smith offered to do so.

"*Most* of him," Maskell confirmed. "Somebody'd come after you left, Mr. Ramsbottom. The coat you'd covered the body with'd been pulled off and the coyotes 'n' turkey vultures had already started feeding. Only, it wasn't neither of them'd cut *both* his hands off."

"That settles it beyond *any* doubt, Al!" Mark exclaimed, as everybody at the table looked down at the black gloves that Smith was still wearing. "*Both* bunches were after *you!*"

"You mean for the bounty that's still offered on him?" Dawn queried.

"Not the way they went at it, honey," the blond giant denied. "Let us not forget that from the beginning, knowing what sent him on the dodge, Freddie 'n' Dusty made certain sure all the posters put out on him always read 'Wanted, *Alive Only.*' They couldn't collect anything after they'd made wolf bait of him. Fact being, they could wind up facing a charge of murder was they to bring him in dead. Top of which, the bunch didn't look like they was aiming to try to take him alive."

"Those yahoos at the river certain sure weren't," Smith asserted. "Was I asked, I'd say both bunches had been told to get me *dead*, and it wasn't the law who did the telling."

"There's a better chance of that being right than of me voting Republican," the sheriff supported. "Way I cut the sign, the jasper who lit a shuck came back after you'd left, Mr. Ramsbottom. Figured on collecting the pay they'd been offered for making wolf bait of you, even though they hadn't. They'd been told to bring your hands to whoever hired 'em to prove the chore'd been done, but not *why*, so he reckoned his *amigo's* would pass for your'n."

"Only, he must've got one hell of a shock when he showed 'em to his boss," Mark assessed. "'Cause I wouldn't say the odds were any too short on his *amigo* having hands like yours, Al."

"It's not real likely he would," Smith replied.

There was a good reason for the certainty both men expressed on the point.

In fact, even in situations when politeness generally required this should be done, Smith had an excellent excuse for refraining from removing his gloves.

Knowing it would cause far more trouble than was desirable under the circumstances if he should have a Texas Ranger—which Smith had been at the time—killed for investigating his affairs, Teodoro Fuentes had adopted less drastic means. Smith having been drugged and taken prisoner, both of his forefingers had been surgically amputated on Fuentes's orders, although there was nothing wrong with them.

"Do you know either of those gents who're just going out, Sheriff?" Smith inquired before anything more could be said on the subject of his mutilated hands.

"Wouldn't go so far's to say I know them," Maskell replied, looking in the required direction. "But I allus try to get acquainted with folks's come into my baili-wick, 'specially when they strike me as being interesting. First time we met, a couple of days back, the one dressed like a gambler told me his name's Lance Sidcup. Allows he's riding shotgun for the other one, Professor Amos Cruikshank."

"Even with a name like *that,*" Smith drawled, watching the pair until they disappeared into the lobby. "What sort of professoring does he do that he needs somebody to ride shotgun on him?"

"That's what I asked Sidcup," the sheriff answered. "Seems he's a professor of mathematics who's come up with a system for winning at various gambling games. Only, it's different from all the others you hear tell about—it *works.* He's done considerable well at it back East, but allows he could need protection against sore losers west of the Big Muddy."

"Hereford doesn't seem a likely place for them to be visiting," Mark put in, also having found the pair inter-esting. "It's never come to be known as a gambling town, so far's I've heard."

"That's what I told 'em," Maskell declared. " 'What little gambling goes on hereabouts is only for small stakes,' I said. Sidcup allowed they wasn't figuring on playing here in town, but were waiting for word to reach them about where they can sit in on a private no-limit poker game. Do you reckon you know them from some-place, Mr. Ramsbottom?"

"Nope, I can't say's I do," Smith admitted. "Would they be staying here at the hotel?"

"Sure," the sheriff confirmed. "Why?"

"I can't bring to mind seeing either of them down here after the shooting last night," Smith replied. "And I got the feeling they was looking me over *real* good while we've been talking."

"What's happened since you came to town, you're like' to get talked about and looked at, even if they didn't come down last night to see what was happening," the sheriff asserted. "Was Sidcup looking this way?"

"Nope," Smith replied. "He'd got his back to us all the time. It was the professor gent who was doing the staring."

"Could be it wasn't *you* he was staring at," Maskell suggested. "He's kind of hard of hearing and watches whoever he's talking too real careful to help him know what's being said."

"Then he was likely doing just that with Sidcup," Smith drawled. "And I could be getting more than just a mite jumpy when there's no call for it."

1. How such establishments operated and threatened to disrupt the economy of Texas is described in THE HIDE AND TALLOW MEN.

12
DO YOUR DUTY, SHERIFF, ARREST HIM

"There's some who'd say you've got good cause to be more than that mite jumpy, way you've been treated since you come back to Texas," Sheriff Maskell asserted. "Anyways, whoever took the hands from the jasper you killed must have come and gone along the trail. We couldn't cut any sign that might help us pick out his hoss."

"I'd know him again, should we meet up," Waxahachie Smith claimed.

"I don't reckon you'll get the chance," Maskell answered. "On the way back, we saw some smoke rising and rid over. Found the burned-out remains of a line cabin and there was a corpse charred beyond recognition inside, along with all that was left of two saddles, bridles, reins, and war bags. Way they were charred up, wasn't nothing to tell who owned them. Wilf hunted 'round outside and found a couple of unsaddled hosses with brands neither of us recognized. Signs were they'd been turned loose by a feller who lit out on another one. I reckon the body's the jasper who cut the hands off the dead 'n', figuring to sell them as your'n to whoever he met. Only, he got paid off in lead, not gold, for trying to cut a rusty with a cold deck. Trouble being, there's no easy way of proving any of it. Whoever did it pulled out along the trail and didn't leave so much as a hoofprint."

"You've never struck me as being a man who wanted everything made easy for him, Tom," Dawn Counter remarked with a smile aroused by the peace officer's apparently disgruntled demeanor.

"Then I've surely struck you wrong," Maskell said. "I'll take *everything* the easiest I can. And, so far, there hasn't been *nothing* easy about this whole game."

"What else's gone wrong?" Dawn inquired, sounding sympathetic.

"Just about everything," the sheriff replied. "Like I said when I got here after the fuss, I can't bring to mind seeing those four jaspers who got shot around town last night. Which means them and the one who got away couldn't've been together in any place Wilf and me looked over while we were making the rounds. There's no way we'd miss seeing that many hired guns in a bunch."

"Could be they kept split up until they figured they'd be needed," Mark suggested. "Was they behaving peaceable, you'd not be so likely to notice just one, or even two of them, in a place."

"I'm not denying it," Maskell agreed. "Town wasn't overbusy last night, but there was enough cowhands in for us to miss them if they was split up and weren't doing anything to make us notice them."

"One thing I do know," Smith asserted. "They didn't ride in just ahead, or close after me. Wondering if those two wasn't just owlhoots after my poke, I laid up clear of the river to make sure there wasn't anybody on my trail.

So I *know* I wasn't being followed, nor had anybody riding point on me."

"Talking of riding, that's something else I don't figure," the sheriff stated. "The three who come in the front had their hosses with their gear ready for leaving town at the hitching rail, but there wasn't any 'round the side, unless the jasper who lit a shuck took them along."

"Happen he did, I didn't hear him," Mark stated. "He was going lickety-split on foot like the Devil after a yearling when he lit out."

"Which don't help me a whole heap," Maskell declared. "'Cause the night hostler down to Whitlock's livery barn can account for every critter in his place, and it was the same at Benteen's. Least, there wasn't any saddled horses inside or 'round back of the barn, and Wilf peeked in the window of the tack room and saw the burro was empty. So they must've been stashed somewhere else."

"It all points that way," Smith conceded, and the blond giant nodded agreement. "So who-all around town would let them do it?"

"Who *could* let them do it?" Mark supplemented. "Even two hosses with the riders' twenty-year gatherings on the saddles around most places, 'cepting maybe saloons and such, would be like' to draw notice."

"Maybe each of them left his horse someplace away from the rest," Dawn suggested. "That way, they wouldn't attract so much notice and, once they'd done the shooting, they'd be harder to hunt down in ones than as a bunch."

"That would mean five hosses, saddled and loaded with all their boss's gear—leastwise, the three out front were, and I reckon the other two'd be just as eager to get going when the shooting was over—each standing someplace until needed," the sheriff commented. "Which they'd have to be somewhere you'd expect to find a horse waiting, or they'd draw as much notice as if they was all together."

"How about on the hitching rail of a saloon?" Dawn offered. "Or outside the house of ill repute, if you've got one, Tom?"

"We've got one, or so I do hear tell," Maskell admitted. "Only, all the saloons were closed and their hitching rails empty by half past eleven, and Mrs. Clinton's place was the same. Leastwise, no matter who-all might be rooming there for the night, there wasn't any hosses outside."

"Something tells me you don't cotton to that Benteen *hombre* who runs the town's other livery barn, Tom," Mark said.

"I don't," Maskell admitted. "He's been trying to get his cousin elected as sheriff. I don't hold *that* against him. It's just that he's a staunch Republican and'd like to have one wearing the badge, 'specially if that one was his cousin."

"He's a horse-trader, too," Dawn remarked. "And not entirely above stooping to sharp practice. In fact, from what I've heard, he doesn't always bother to stoop."

"Well, I've never *caught* him doing nothing dishonest," the sheriff declared. "And, knowing him, I don't see him taking the risk of letting those fellers leave their hosses at his barn. He'd figure that'd be one of the first places I'd go looking for them."

"Comes to liking and not liking," Mark drawled, "I got the notion you don't exactly look on the undertaker as a friend."

"You've got the right notion," Maskell confirmed. "Him and Benteen are tarred with the same brush."

"Business partners?" Mark queried.

"Not on a share-and-share-alike basis, so far as I know," the sheriff replied. "But their bunch got a civic ordinance put on the books that the property of any stranger who dies anywhere in the county gets sold to pay off whatever debts he might have run up and for the burying. As coroner, Jones the Burial handles the whole thing, and it's always Benteen who winds up with whatever's going at a price that'll show him a profit."

"Talking of strangers dying, Tom," Smith remarked, "I reckon's how, if those fellers we made wolf bait of'd've had anything to say who they was, or what they was doing hereabouts, on 'em or in their gear, you'd have said so."

"They didn't, or I would have," Maskell replied.

Before anything more could be said on the subject, the undertaker arrived with five other men. Two were big, heavily built, clad in good-quality clothing, and had a strong family resemblance. The third was small, skinny, soberly attired, and rat-faced. Clad in cheap and dirty range-style garments, the pair bringing up the rear each had a Colt revolver tucked into the waistband of his trousers. Despite their attire, neither looked like a cowhand. Rather, they struck the Counters and Smith as being the kind of loafers to be found in any cattle-country town, and it was a surprise to see them in such company.

"Do you know who this man is, Sheriff?" Jones asked, louder than was necessary and gesturing at Smith as the group came to a halt in a loose half-circle.

"Mr. Counter told me he's Mr. Aloysius W. Ramsbottom the Third when we met up last night," the peace officer replied.

"Then Mr. Counter tol—must have heard *wrong,*" the undertaker stated, making the amendment when he realized his original words would be tantamount to calling the blond giant a liar, an accusation he knew would be most unwise. "That isn't his name. He's Waxahachie Smith, and there is an outstanding warrant for his arrest."

"Are you *sure?*" Maskell asked.

"I'm willing to verify it," Hugo Benteen asserted, his face showing what could have been righteous virtue. "So do your duty, Sheriff. Arrest him!"

"Would there be a reward for doing it?" Maskell queried.

"There would, for a thousand dollars," Benteen confirmed with relish. "And it goes to whoever causes him to be arrested."

"Which's *you,*" Maskell drawled. "I never took you gents for bounty hunters."

"And we're not," Jones asserted, noticing that the conversation was attracting the attention of everybody else in the room. While willing to help discredit the sheriff and take his share of the reward, he realized how the stigma of the suggestion could have an adverse effect upon his political aspirations. "We want to see the law is upheld regardless of whose friend might be involved." He gestured to the man with the family resemblance to Benteen and continued, "If *you* won't take him in, Mr. Ragland is willing to make a citizen's arrest. This man is wanted—!"

"I just knowed this would happen!" Smith interrupted in tones that implied exasperation. "Are *you* satisfied I'm who Mr. Counter said, Sheriff?"

"I'm not!" Jones put in before the peace officer could reply.

"Or me," Benteen supported.

"That's all I need to know," Smith announced. "You do what these two good law-abiding gents want, Sheriff, and I won't hold you to blame for what comes next. Would there be a lawyer in town?"

"There's Colonel Fothergill," Maskell replied, wondering what was coming and refraining from mentioning that the fourth member of the group before them was qualified for the designation.

"Could you send for him to meet us down to the

jail?" Smith requested. "I'll be needing him to act for me."

"Then you admit that you're Waxahachie Smith?" the undertaker asked in a triumphant voice.

"You pair said that, not me," Smith corrected. "So it's *you* and not the sheriff's'll stand for the consequences."

" 'Consequences'?" Benteen repeated with a frown.

"If that's a threat, look you—!" Jones commenced, speaking much louder than was necessary, and the hands of the two loafers reached to the butts of their Colts.

"Call it a friendly warning," Smith corrected, continuing to sit with his hands resting on the table. Although his main attention was directed toward the group of men standing before him, beyond them he could see that Sidcup and Cruikshank had halted on the stairway leading to the upper floors and were watching. "If I suffer the embarrassment of being arrested in front of all these folks and taken to the pokey through your doing, well, I reckon Colonel Forthergill'll agree with me I'm within my lawful 'n' Constitutional rights to sue you both under Article Eleven, Twenty-three, Sixty-one of the United States Legal Code, which same covers causing the false arrest of an innocent and law-abiding citizen."

"Can you explain that for us, Mr. Ramsbottom," Maskell requested when Lawyer Cyrus Comstay did not make any comment.

"Why, sure," Smith obliged. "These gentlemen are accusing me of being a wanted owlhoot and demanding you take me to the pokey on that account. Which is same's false arrest, and I'm allowed to sue whoever caused it to happen."

"Would that be the legal law, *Counselor* Comstay?" Maskell inquired, his manner indicating the expectation of an answer in the affirmative.

"Well—well—!" the lawyer began, unwilling to admit

that he had never heard of the United States Legal Code. However, it had been quoted with a most convincing air of authority by one who appeared to be fully conversant with its ramifications, and he knew that in some circumstances it was possible for a lawsuit for false arrest to be brought against those responsible. "I—I—!"

"Are you saying you're *not* Waxahachie Smith?" Jones demanded, directing a bitter scowl at Comstay.

"It's more that you pair are saying I *am*," Smith countered.

"But your fing—!" the undertaker began, and pointed at the tabletop. "Take those gloves off and show us your hands."

"I can show you something a whole heap more convincing than that," Smith claimed without changing his position. "If one of you gents will reach into my jacket's inside pocket and take out my wallet—!"

Despite the eagerness they had originally displayed to make the sheriff perform his duty—or refuse and supply a reason to be used against him at the forthcoming election for the office—none of the group did as they were requested.

"Shall I do it, Mr. Ramsbottom?" Dawn inquired.

"If you'd be so kind, ma'am," Smith authorized.

Producing the wallet, the woman carried on doing as she was instructed. Opening it, she extracted a photograph and an envelope from which she removed a single sheet of paper. Accepting the first item, Maskell studied it and then showed it to Jones, Benteen, and Ragland, but not the loafers. Startled exclamations burst from all of them at what they saw. There were three male figures in the photograph. In the center was a tall, well-built, and impressive-looking man. However, the group gave him barely a glance. Their attention was devoted to the other two men. To the right, dressed as he was at that moment except that he was not wearing his gloves, was the man they had demanded be arrested. On the left, wearing the attire of a working cowhand from Texas, with the badge of a peace officer on his vest and also displaying his hands, the third figure was slightly smaller. However, apart from having a heavy mustache, he looked very much like Smith. The resemblance extended to both having lost the forefinger from each hand.

"Maybe one of those gents would like to read the affidavit Mrs. Counter's holding?" Smith suggested, giving no sign of how he regarded the consternation caused the group by the photograph.

"Go to it, Counselor Comstay," Maskell prompted.

" 'To whom it may concern,' " the lawyer began, having accepted the paper reluctantly and found it was a typewritten document. Such machines were still far from common on the open-range country west of the Mississippi River, and therefore it was even more impressive and official-looking. " 'This is to clarify the situation for Aloysius W. Ramsbottom the Third, resident of our city, in case he needs to offer proof of his identity while visiting Texas. Bravely going to help a family cut off from town in a blizzard last year, he suffered frostbite that caused the loss of his forefingers. Knowing of his affliction and, in addition to both being Texans, realizing there is some physical resemblance between them that the injuries has increased, Waldo 'Waxahachie' Smith, our town marshal, is desirous of preventing a mistake being made where their respective identities are concerned. For this purpose, they were photographed together in my presence. We ask all peace officers and others to take note of our statement that the bearer is Aloysius W. Ramsbottom the Third, and not Waldo "Waxahachie" Smith.' "

"Is that *real?*" Jones asked, his bearing indicative of disbelief.

"It's signed by and bears the official seal of office of Mayor W.S.B. Jeffreys of Widows Creek, Wyoming Ter-

ritory, and has been notarized by a local attorney,"
Comstay answered, looking uncomfortable and refusing
to meet anybody else's eyes. "So I see no cause to doubt
its authenticity."

"Then it looks like you've made a real bad mistake,
Mr. Jones, Mr. Benteen," Maskell commented, needing
all his ability as a poker player to conceal his elation at
this most unexpected turn of events. Retrieving the document and photograph from Comstay's limp fingers, he
went on, "This letter and picture satisfies *me*. Still, if
you gents still want me to arrest Mr. Ramsbottom on
your behalf, that's what I'll do. Only, was you to ask *my*
opinion, I wouldn't reckon, with evidence like he's got,
you'd have a chance of avoiding heavy damages when he
takes you afore the judge to answer for having him arrested. What do you say, Counselor?"

"I don't think there is any need for Mr.—Ramsbottom to be arrested," Comstay stated. "But I'm sure Mr.
Jones and Mr. Benteen acted in good faith."

"I know it sounds sort of hard to believe two fellers
could look so alike, have the same kind of damage done
to their hands, and find themselves in the same town,"
Smith asserted with an air of magnanimity that seemed
sincere. "But it happened. So, unless you want to take it
any further, I won't hold it against you gents for making
the mistake and doing your duty as upright, law-abiding
citizens."

Jones and Benteen exchanged baffled and angry
glances. Far from having achieved the purpose that had
brought them to the hotel, each realized he was faced
with a situation likely to cause him the loss of a considerable sum of money. Having no liking for either of
them, not only would Colonel Fothergill take the greatest delight in being presented with the opportunity to
prosecute them, with the evidence Smith could present
and the backing of a man as important as Mark
Counter, they were liable to find themselves compelled

to pay heavy damages as well as the other costs incurred by the trial.[1]

"W-we made a mistake!" Jones announced bitterly, sounding as if the words were leaving a sour taste in his mouth. "Forget what's happened, Sheriff."

Swinging on his heel without waiting for a reply, the undertaker led something closer to a rush away than a dignified departure. Not until they had gone and the interrupted activities of the other occupants of the room were resumed did Smith remove his hands from the top of the table.

"Way you sat so still all the time they was here, Mr. Ramsbottom," Maskell remarked, "you looked like you was making sure nobody'd reckon you was going to get so riled with them you'd need stopping."

"I've heard tell of such things happening," Smith admitted. "So I got to thinking's how somebody could've read the signs wrong and figured to help you by throwing down on me did I make a move's could be reckoned was hostile."

"Do you have anybody special in mind?" the sheriff asked.

"Nobody's I'd want to name, 'specially as I don't know their names," Smith replied. "Could be I'm getting all edgy for no reason."

"There's some might say's how you'd got cause for it, what's happened since you hit town," Maskell claimed. Then he gestured with the document he was still holding and went on in a neutral tone, "This *is* genuine, isn't it?"

"Why, sure," Smith declared. "Leastwise, although I'll have to come right out and fess up that the rest of it's a mite shy of the truth, the signature and seal of the mayor are real enough."

"But it's been notarized as the truth by a local lawyer," the sheriff pointed out, sounding disapproving for the first time.

"Not what's said in the letter," Smith corrected. "If you look, which none of them knobheads did, you'll see Counselor Stableford states he's only confirming it's got Mayor Jeffreys's signature and official seal. We figured I might need some help should I be recognized and arrested on that old warrant, so we came up with the story 'bout how 'Aloysius W. Ramsbottom the Third' came to have the same kind of damage done to his hands as Waxahachie Smith, who he looks so much like."

"There's some'd say that's kind of sneaky," Maskell claimed with a grin after ascertaining that he had been told the truth with regard to the exact wording of the affidavit. "But this picture's got me kissed off against the cushion. I've come to know you're mighty slick, Mr. Ramsbottom, but I wouldn't reckon even *you* could be in two places at the same time."

"Nor was I, regardless of the way it seems," Smith admitted after glancing around as if to make sure he would not be overheard. In passing, he noticed that the two men who had aroused his interest earlier were walking up the stairs toward the second floor. "We concluded's how the letter might not be enough, so one of Wil—Mayor Jeffreys's kin, a right smart young feller name of George Eastman who's visiting from back East, made it for us. He took a picture of me wearing those range clothes and sporting a false mustache, and I'll be switched if I wasn't looking a mite shorter than on another he got of me dressed like I am now and with my *amigo,* Deputy Marhsal C. B. Frith, because we figured he looked more like folks's didn't know would expect a mayor to look than Wil Jeffreys does. Don't ask me how George did it, but he's sure enough a whing-ding when it comes to handling a camera, and 'fore you could shake a stick, he'd given me this picture of 'Marshal Waxahachie Smith,' 'His Honor, Mayor W.S.B. Jeffreys,' and 'Aloyius W. Ramsbottom the Third' standing in a line."[2]

"It fooled them—and me," the sheriff commented with genuine admiration.

"I'm right pleased to hear it," Smith stated, accepting the document and picture. "Is there something else worrying you?"

"How's about that Act from the United States Legal Code's you quoted so knowing?" Maskell asked. "I've been a peace officer 'most all my grown-up life and figure to know my job, but I don't recollect ever having heard of such a thing."

"Way he looked, 'cepting he wouldn't come right out flat-footed and admit it with so many folks listening, neither had that rat-faced li'l law wrangler they had along," Smith assessed. "Which could be because I made up both the Act and its number. To save you asking, the last's my birth date and makes the whole thing sound even more impressive."

"Like I said, *real* sneaky," Maskell declared, but the timbre of the words suggested praise and not condemnation. "Meaning no offense, Wax—Mr. Ramsbottom, but, one way and another, I'll not be oversorry to see you pull out."

"Something tells me you won't be alone in that," Smith answered. "And, what's come off since I hit your bailiwick, I hope you don't mind me saying's how I'm one of 'em. Hard's it is to *believe,* I've come 'round to he notion there're folks hereabouts as don't *like* lovable li'l ole me. Which being, unless you want me to be moving on sooner, I reckon I'll be heading down to Brownsville to handle some business 'round noon tomorrow."

"That'll do fine," the sheriff drawled. "Only, I'd be right obliged if you didn't have nobody else come around trying to kill you afore then."

"I'll try not to let it happen until after I'm over the Deaf Smith County line," the reddish-haired Texan promised solemnly.

"One thing I like," Maskell declared in just as seemingly a serious fashion, "is an obliging gent like you. I'm only pleased there aren't more of 'em around."

1. *How costly such a mistake could be even without the case going to court is told in* Part Four, "The Penalty of False Arrest," MARK COUNTER'S KIN.
2. *Why Waxahachie Smith thought Deputy Town Marshal C. B. Frith would seem more convincing in the role of Mayor W.S.B. Jeffreys is explained in* SLIP GUN.

13
DON'T TRY TO CUT IN ON
MY GAME

Never a cheerful man, while walking through the darkness in the direction of the property that served as his home and place of business, Jones the Burial was in an even more doleful frame of mind than usual. This had come about as a result of an unpleasant discussion he had just concluded with Hugo Benteen. Despite the matter having been arrived at by mutual discussion and agreement, each had sought to lay the blame on the other for what had happened at the Cattlemen's Hotel that morning and, particularly, during its aftermath.

Being of a mutually parsimonious nature, neither the undertaker nor the owner of the livery stable had been pleased when Lawyer Comstay demanded a fee for his "legal services" and realized he knew far too much about their mutual less-than-legitimate affairs for a refusal to be advisable. The pair were less enamored of the two loafers hired to play a part in the scheme who insisted on receiving a sum of money apiece so they could get out of town in case Sheriff Maskell or, more particularly, Ramsbottom—who had proven to be a deadly hand with a gun even though it seemed he was not Waxahachie Smith—guessed what they were supposed to do given the slightest excuse.

Wondering how he might get his revenge on the pair of loafers should they return, or if it might be advisable to arrange for this never to happen by having them killed, Jones had the thoughts jolted from his head. He was passing the end of a building when a hand caught him by the scruff of the neck. Before he could react in any way, he was swung in a half-circle to be slammed backward against the hard boards of the wall. Dazed by the impact, he was unable to resist as the grasp was transferred to his throat and he stared at a human shape that loomed before him. Because of the surrounding gloom, he could tell no more than that the man responsible for the attack was tall. A Stetson hat was tilted so the brim concealed his face, and a long slicker covered the rest of his garments in a way that avoided any hint of what they—and, through them, he—might be.

"Just what damned fool game were you and that lard-gutted son of a bitch, Benteen, trying to pull at the Cattlemen's this morning?" growled a harsh voice that the undertaker had heard before without being any more certain on the two previous occasions than now of what the speaker might look like.

When he had been summoned by the unknown man for a second meeting, Jones had tried to discover with whom he was dealing. However, the Chinese helper he had given orders to trail and learn where the man could be located had returned much later than anticipated, having been knocked unconscious before the desired information could be found. He had brought a message, which was left in his hand, that gave a dire warning against such tactics being employed in the event of further contact being made.

"We were going to have the feller you said was Waxahachie Smith arrested—!" the undertaker began.

"Or gunned down when he refused to go quietly?" the dark shape said in a mocking tone.

"That *could* have happened," Jones admitted truthfully, albeit resentfully, since the failure of the scheme had cost him more money than its successful conclusion would have.

"And *you* could have the brains of a louse, but I doubt it," the man snarled. "Neither of those knuckleheads you'd got with you could have got their guns clear before Smith, Counter, or the sheriff took them out. What's more, knowing they'd have spilled their guts about what you and Benteen wanted doing if they'd been taken alive, I'd have made sure neither of them could and, as I don't reckon either of you would be any more staunch comes to being questioned, I'd have made sure you couldn't say anything that might lead to me either."

"You wouldn't have *dared*—!" Jones began, but his voice lacked conviction.

"Folks have been shot down 'accidentally' by somebody wanting to help out the law before now, and likely will again," the man pointed out. "And I don't reckon the sheriff's so all-fired fond of you and Benteen that he'd look too closely into how it happened to you. The thing is, from now on, don't try to cut in on *my* game."

"You haven't been doing too well at it, look you," the undertaker reminded sullenly, trying without success to remember who had been close enough in the dining room to carry out the threat. "From what I hear, *your* men missed twi—!"

"For the money your bunch is paying, I can't get topgrade help," the man declared, bringing the other's words to a halt by tightening the grip on his throat.

"And talking of money, I want two thousand bucks to cover expenses."

"T-t-two *thousand* bu—*dollars?*" Jones gabbled as the fingers loosened their hold a trifle.

When the undertaker had become involved with a group of liberal-radical politicians at Austin because he had thought it might prove advantageous to his aspirations, he had not expected to find himself engaged in their activities to any great extent. Therefore, it had been a shock when the man had given him a letter from their leader demanding he render every kind of assistance that might be required. Although the writer did not mention the subject, he knew the group was aware of various things about him that he had no desire to be made public and he felt sure would be if he refused to comply in any way. What was more, he had been told enough to realize that his unwelcome visitor was also privy to his secrets.

"That'll cover things nicely," the man said calmly. "I'll come with you and take it now. Or would you rather it came out that you'd let the fellers who tried to kill Counter and Smith at the hotel hide at your place until it was time for them to make the try?"

"*You* told me to do it!" Jones croaked, having taken it for granted that—as his Chinese employees, only one of whom spoke English and, being a highly ranked member of the criminal tong from which they were hired, would not betray him—there was no way the sheriff could have learned what he had done.

"Only, *you* don't know who I am, or where to find me," the man reminded dryly. "So you'd best pay up like I said."

"I—I don't have so much money—!" the undertaker gasped.

"Like hell you don't. You've made plenty out of the deal you've got going with Benteen for selling the belongings of strangers who died in the county," the man cut in. "Your kind won't have more than a small deposit in the bank and the rest'll be hid somewhere around your home. So I'll come and let you fetch it out to me, then you can get Benteen to pay his share when you see him next. Don't get worried, though. This is the last money I'll be after from you. I'm not going to try anything else against Smith here in town."

"He's got proof that he isn't Waxahachie Smith," Jones claimed sullenly as the fingers left his throat.

"Be that as it may," the man answered, showing no sign of being worried by the information. "No matter who he is, he's still the one who's being sent to fetch Frank Smith. Only, when they get together, I'll be around to make sure that there's no cure found for the Texas fever."

After his wife had had dinner and retired for the night, Mark Counter spent the remainder of the evening with Waxahachie Smith in the bar at the Cattlemen's Hotel. Doing so allowed them to make the acquaintance of the two men from the East who had aroused Smith's interest shortly before the attempt to have him arrested. Having repeated the information about themselves supplied to the sheriff on their arrival at Hereford, except for ascertaining that the Texans were not prospects as possible competitors at gambling, neither Easterner had shown even the smallest amount of curiosity over their presence in the town, which would have been permissible under the accepted conventions of the West. What was more, when the blond giant had brought up the matter of the thwarted attack upon himself and Ramsbottom, the professor claimed to have been so tired from working upon his system that he had slept through the disturbance. Sidcup excused his failure to appear downstairs by stating that he had not considered the disturbance to be any of his business and had remained in his room.

In spite of the explanation he was given for the pair being absent, Smith had taken the opportunity to study them carefully. He concluded that Sidcup was intelligent, tough, and probably counted upon ability with a gun rather than trying to make a living out of gambling. It was understandable that such a man might be disinclined to investigate even a serious incident that did not concern him. Cruikshank seemed mild and harmless, excusing an occasional failure to respond immediately when addressed by either Texan, his explanation being that he was somewhat hard of hearing.

Doing as he had told Sheriff Maskell regarding his future movements, having continued to spread the rumor that he was meaning to go to transact some business in Brownsville, Smith had remained in the town until the time quoted. When taking his departure, he had ridden in the appropriate direction and was escorted as far as the Deaf Smith County line by Deputy Sheriff Wilf Piggot. As an added precaution against his being followed too closely, having left the mares to be serviced by Tolly Maxwell's stallion, the cowhands brought from the MC by the Counters had trailed them at a distance of about two miles until they parted.

Covering the miles he was traversing at a reasonable rate without imposing too great a strain upon his two horses, to keep to the pretense that he was making for Brownsville, the reddish-haired Texan continued to travel in a southeasterly direction for two days. Then, having passed through Tulia, still moving at the same pace, he swung eastward since this was the true direction he was going. While in the town he commenced a practice he meant to follow as long as he remained in Texas by calling upon the sheriff of Swisher County. Being shown the "evidence" purporting to prove that despite the resemblance to the description of Waxahachie Smith he was "Aloysius W. Ramsbottom the Third," the

peace officer accepted it without question on being informed that he was merely passing through the region.

Although the journey so far was uneventful, it seemed
that the precautions taken by Smith when leaving Hereford might not have proved entirely successful. All the
time he was moving, he kept a careful watch on his rear.
On the midafternoon of the fifth day, having spent the
night at Wichita Falls and now traveling toward Henri-
etta in Clay County, he saw a small cloud of dust rising
at a distance. Not only was it still there twenty-four
hours later, it was somewhat closer and, with the aid of
a powerful telescope taken from his saddlebags, he
made out the cause to be a group of five riders. The
distance was still too great for him to see anything more
than this basic fact. However, he knew there was no
danger of their reaching him before nightfall, and he
saw no reason to go faster. With that in mind, he could
safely find a secure spot in which to bed down for the
night, and should the need arise, he would decide how
to deal with the situation.

"Where the hell're the hosses?"

Uttered in tones redolent of fury, the words aroused
the other four men who were sleeping on the ground
around the gray ashes of a burned-out fire in a clearing
where they had made camp the previous evening. Like
the speaker, they wore grubby range clothing and were
well armed. Regardless of their attire, none were cowhands. They had been hired to follow and kill Waxahachie Smith. However, the delay caused by the precautions he had taken prevented them from catching up
with him. Therefore, at sundown, they had halted the
pursuit with the intention of taking it up in the morning.

"Looks like they've gone," remarked the oldest of the
group dryly as he and the rest got to their feet.

Although he had been a hired gun for all his grown
life, Milt Carver had never ranked high among his kind.

On the other hand, he had developed a streak of caution that kept him alive long after a great many of his more skillful and less wary contemporaries were dead. Because they had been acquainted in the past, he had been selected by Pampa to supply up-to-date information and help recruit the assistance that was required. On learning against whom they would be in contention, he had avoided being involved in any active participation at Austin. Then, having taken over as go-between for the unknown employer after Pampa was killed, he had gathered reinforcements. Before he arrived with the group who followed Mark Counter to Hereford, the man who hired him had tried to bring about Smith's death by giving the chore to Monte Parker. Knowing that the failure strengthened his own position, Carver had been pleased on learning the result of the attempt.

Having hidden at Jones the Burial's place when the abortive attempt to gun down the blond giant and Ramsbottom took place, Carver joined the survivors when they made good their escape. At a prearranged rendezvous just outside the town, receiving fresh orders from the still-unknown man and a thousand dollars to cover whatever expenses were entailed, he had gone to where the pair and two more who were waiting in a disused cabin some miles away. Because of the precaution taken by Ramsbottom, they were delayed in following him. The chance occurrence of going to Tulia for fresh mounts warned them that Smith had changed directions. By the time they were approaching Wichita Falls, Carver had concluded that their quarry was not making for Brownsville. However, despite also riding a two-horse relay apiece, they still were not close enough to take any action when they made camp for the night.

From the beginning of their acquaintance, Carver had no liking for any of the men with whom he was traveling, and their mutually condescending attitude toward him had done nothing to bring about a change of mind.

None were half his age, and despite realizing that he alone knew how to contact their employer, they had continued to make it clear that they considered him to be along merely on sufferance. Not only had they done much complaining over the time the pursuit was taking, they had repeatedly refused to adopt the basic precautions he had suggested. His suggestion that they should take turns to mount guard through the night was greeted with derision. Furthermore, they had been drinking before bedding down, and Carver could not resist the temptation to join them.

"How the hell did they get loose?" demanded the youngest of the group. "I tethered *mine* good."

"Goddamn it!" snarled another of the party as they went to where the animals had been standing. "They've been *cut* loose and led off!"

"Do you reckon that son of a bitch we're trailing come back and done it?" inquired the youngest.

"Nope!" Carver asserted with such conviction that the rest looked at him. Bending, he picked up two objects that none of others had noticed lying on the ground. "Doing it'd take an Injun."

"Injun!" snorted the second speaker, oozing derision. "There ain't been no Injuns hereabouts for years."

"Somebody must've forgot to tell this one," Carver claimed, holding out the objects he had retrieved.

"They's just a pair of wored-out old moccasins," the youngest growled.

"Yep, that they be," Carver agreed. "And they was left by a *Comanch'.*"

"A Comanch'?" the biggest of the party snorted. "They've all been on the reservation for the last twenty years or more."

"Back in the old days," Carver explained, showing no sign of having heard the comment, "when a Comanch' helped hisself to hosses, he used to leave a wored-out pair of moccasins behind to let the owners know's how he didn't need 'em 'cause he wouldn't be walking no more. Only, it didn't end there."

"What else?" the youngest asked, remembering all the stories he had heard about the ferocity and fighting ability of the Comanche Indians.

"It also means he's giving word's how he don't want nobody coming after the hosses," Carver elaborated somberly, thinking back to a time when he had seen a pair of old moccasins left behind and remembered who had done so. He was also all too aware of with whom the man responsible was closely connected and did not care for the possibilities arising from his conclusions. "Should they do it, he'll get more'n a mite riled and stop them cold."[1]

"That ain't going to stop *me* going after him!" the biggest hard case declared.

"That's up to you," Carver replied as the rest signaled agreement with the statement. Waving a hand in a southerly direction, he went on, "The sign heads off that way. I'll see you gents around."

"Aren't you coming with us?" the youngster asked.

"Nope, I'm headed for Wichita Falls," Carver replied, knowing he could send an apparently innocent telegraph message at the town that nevertheless would inform the man who had hired him of the latest development and request instructions. "Because I've got a sneaky notion who *this* Comanch' is and, gents, there's no way's I'm going to get *him* riled up at me!"

1. *The incident is described in* OLD MOCCASINS ON THE TRAIL.

14
MR. SMITH, MEET
MR. SMITH

Walking along a passageway left between the rows of wooden pens into some of which cattle were being transferred from the railroad cars designed for their shipment, Waxahachie Smith was far from being at ease over the change circumstances had compelled him to make to his means of self-protection.

As the rusty-haired Texan did not possess any official status to serve as an excuse in his still-retained persona as Aloysius W. Ramsbottom the Third, he had taken into account that wearing a handgun or carrying his Colt Lightning rifle openly would not be permissible while he was staying in Chicago.

Wishing to avoid the problems that might otherwise have arisen, including the possibility of causing embarrassment for the senior local police officer whose cooperation had been arranged by Dusty Fog,[1] Smith had left his gunbelt in the carpetbag when he set out for the appointed rendezvous that morning. Nor would carrying his Colt Lightning rifle be any more admissible within the bounds of such a large Eastern city. Nevertheless, because he was disinclined to leave himself without a weapon on his person, the Colt slip gun was tucked into the waistband of his trousers behind his back and concealed by his jacket. It was the first time in well over ten years that he had been compelled to behave in such a fashion, and although he arrived at the Windy City without further attempts upon his life, or even being followed so far as he knew, he still remained wary and on the alert.

Even though there had been no arrangements made for him to carry his armament readily accessible for immediate use during the latter part of the journey, especially in his present locale, Smith had been helped on his way by the arrangements that had been made to facilitate his traveling. Excellent horses as replacements for his own mounts were awaiting him at livery stables on a list that Mark Counter had given to him while discussing the route he was to follow in the privacy of his room at the Cattlemen's Hotel on the night before he left Hereford. Nor was this restricted to the Lone Star State. Making use of friendships formed while he was leading Company C of the Texas Light Cavalry there during the War Between the States,[2] Dusty had arranged for the same facilities to be available while Smith was crossing Arkansas. Arriving at Little Rock, he left the latest pair of animals and his saddles with the man to whom he had been directed. He had ceased wearing his gunbelt, doing so would no longer be practical, since he was continuing the journey by train, although he had taken his slip gun and Colt Lightning along, the latter in its saddle boot.

No matter what means of transport he was using, the time passing without further dangerous developments, Smith had remained constantly vigilant so as to be ready to cope with any further attempts upon his life. None had been made, and it seemed he had thrown his enemies off his trail. Nevertheless, aware that he was in contention against ruthless men with many sources for obtaining information, he was too experienced to allow a false sense of security to dull his perceptions. As a precaution in case his destination had been suspected and arrangements made by his enemies for his reception at Chicago, he kept a careful watch for anything that might be attempted. He followed the instructions he had received in a letter that morning at the hotel into which he had been booked before arriving two days earlier so as to make contact with the man he had traveled so far to meet.

While he had not forgotten that there could still be threats to his well-being, the rusty-haired Texan was paying little attention to what was happening around him as he approached the place where he was to be taken to meet the man whose protection was to be his duty. In addition to the usual noises to be expected at any railroad depot were some that were particular to the kind of area through which he was starting to pass. Only partially domesticated in the first place, the cattle brought in on the train were far from soothed by having been forced to enter the special cars and transported in such a fashion from a trail-end town in Kansas. Nor, if the furious bellows that rang out were any indication, was their temper improved on being urged to emerge and enter the pens.

Under more peaceable conditions, Smith might have found the sights about him of interest. As it was, while walking along, he merely noticed that to his left there were a large number of cattle being allowed to leave the train in which they had been brought from a railroad town in Kansas after having been delivered there by a trail-drive crew. The work was mainly being carried out by what were poorly dressed Easterners, if their clothing and occasional speech were any guide. However, near where the rusty-haired Texan was approaching, they were supplanted by half a dozen cowhands whose attire was indicative of their having come from one of the northern of the cattle-raising states.

Clearly business had been good recently, for only one of the pens at the other side of the passageway was occupied. It was farther along the line and held only a single large longhorn that, going by the noises it was making, possessed an even worse disposition than was usual for its kind. Three men in Eastern garb of a better quality than that worn by the workers around the train were in its immediate vicinity. However, although it seemed likely that they were responsible for the animal's ill temper, he was unable to see what any of them were doing and felt that this was not any of his concern unless one should prove to be the person he was seeking.

Suddenly, Smith's thoughts were jolted from the problem of locating the man he had been sent to contact. Mingled with the awesome bawl of an angry longhorn whose masculine condition had not been changed when the beast had been turned into a steer and the drumming of rapidly approaching hooves, yells of warning came to his ears. Glancing over his shoulder, he found that his guess regarding the cause of the commotion had been correct. Somehow, the solitary animal on the right side of the passageway had escaped from its pen and was charging toward him.

Nor, Smith suspected, had the animal's attaining of freedom been caused by accident. As the massive beast was emerging through the gate, which opened outward and offered him some protection, one of the men who now stood beyond it pressed the glowing end of his cigar against something and made a tossing motion. In an instant, there began a series of rapid bangs accompanied by flashes of flame of the kind the rusty-haired

Texan had seen occur when Chinese workers were cele-
brating the New Year festivities with use of what they
called fireworks. Any longhorn would have been dangerous enough under the circumstances, but this was a
particularly large and, going by appearances, thoroughly
irate bull. Nor was the extent of its already vile temper
lessened by the explosions taking place so close behind
its rump. What was more, in addition to viewing Smith
as a potential impediment to its flight, it gave indications that it was intending to vent its anger upon him.

Even though he had spent little of his working life as
a cowhand, like most people who had grown up in range
country, Smith knew that a longhorn had no fear what-
soever of a man on foot, so he was all too aware of his
peril. Even without the inducement of the provocation
it had received, a bull such as was coming toward him
would prove a dangerous antagonist for even a Texas
flathead grizzly bear to tackle. With that thought in
mind, he reacted fast. While he was doing so, he realized the full extent of his danger under the prevailing
conditions. Effective as the multi-ball loading he generally used in his slip gun undoubtedly was at close range
against a human being, the balls would not have sufficient stopping power to halt the charge. Receiving some
of them in the face might cause the bull to swerve aside,
but they were more likely to increase its fury and make
it determined to take revenge upon him.

While these thoughts were flashing through Smith's
head, his training as a gunfighter caused him to react
instinctively. Unfortunately, when his right hand started
to perform the movements that would have brought out
the slip gun, it was in the fashion that had become second nature to him since the loss of his forefingers.
Therefore, all he managed was to brush the back of his
hand against the waist belt.

The familiar staghorn grips of the handle were not in
their usual position waiting to be enfolded.

In the stress of the moment, Smith had forgotten that his changed circumstances had caused him to make an alteration to the way he was carrying the Colt.

Before Smith could fully appreciate the latest development, he saw something that handed him almost as much of a surprise as had the charging bull.

Wearing clothing similar to that of the other cowhands present, a tall and well-built young Negro had been helping to guide the animals into the pens. He was performing this task while walking along the top rails. However, on seeing what was happening, he responded with most praiseworthy promptitude. Dropping the metal-tipped prod he had been using, he darted, despite having on the typical high-heeled and sharp-toed footwear of his trade, along the narrow wooden plank he was currently occupying with the speed of a high-wire artist performing in a circus.

Throwing himself from the top of the pen, the Negro struck the bull. On making the contact, showing a speed that suggested he had performed a similar feat on a number of occasions, he passed his right arm over the animal's neck and clasped his hand on its nostrils. At the same instant, his left hand closed around the tip of the left horn. Swinging forward his feet and allowing the full weight of his obviously powerful body to lunge downward against his left elbow, he twisted the neck of his captive. Taken unawares and treated in such a fashion, the animal was thrown off balance and went down with its assailant lying on top and retaining the holds.

The impact of the bull's unexpected descent upon the hard ground jarred all the air from its lungs and dazed it, but only momentarily. After a few seconds it started to struggle, and by all appearances, powerful though he undoubtedly was, the Negro would not be able to hold it down. Realizing this, Smith made adjustments to his right hand's position that allowed him to bring the Colt from beneath his jacket. It was his intention to step in close enough to place the muzzle against the animal's forehead and rely upon the three balls in the load having the velocity at such close quarters to drive through the bone into the brain.

"Hold hard there, Mr. Smith!" the Negro yelled, guessing what the rusty-haired Texan had in mind. "Ain't no call for *that!*"

Before the rusty-haired Texan could comment upon the words, or do more than realize he had been addressed by his name, he saw the five white cowhands who had also been helping load the cattle into the stock cars running up. Two of them held coiled ropes and, drawing near, another yelled for the Negro to "get clear, Sam!" Releasing his hold, Smith's rescuer rolled away with alacrity.

As the liberated bull began to rise, a loop was tossed over its head from each side and drawn tight about its neck. Working swiftly in concert with the Negro who had risen, the other cowhands made two groups that grabbed the trailing stem of each rope. Their combined weight was only just sufficient to hold the animal in check as it surged to its feet. However, showing an alacrity that indicated they had performed similar tasks in the past, some of the Eastern workers arrived to help compel it to enter the gate of the nearest empty pen instead of the one it had vacated. Once there, its forelegs were ensnared and it was toppled to the ground for long enough to allow the nooses around its neck to be removed. With this done, all but the man who did the roping got out swiftly. On reaching the passageway, the last to emerge wasted no time before closing the entrance. Having released the animal, the roper followed them and climbed over the fence so swiftly that the bull was unable to rise in time to attack him.

"*Gracias,* friend," Smith said to his first rescuer, returning the Colt to its carrying position beneath his jacket. "You got here just in time."

"I'm right pleased I was able to, boss," the Negro replied, and glanced along the passageway to the pen from which the bull had been released. "Blast it, though, *they* managed to light a shuck when what was doing, 'stead of coming to land a hand with their critter."

"I'd say you know a whole heap more than we want to talk about here," the rusty-haired Texan asserted, and turned his attention to the white cowhands and Easterners before any reply could be made. *"Gracias* to you gents for helping out."

" 'Tis all part of the railroad's service," the biggest of the Easterners replied in an Irish brogue. "And now we'd best be getting back to unloading the darlin' little beasts afore the boss comes wanting to know why we're slacking 'stead of doing the work we're always getting told we're so well paid to do."

"I surely like a man who's loyal to his boss," Smith said with a grin when he was left with only the cowhands, none of whom appeared to share the sentiments regarding a resumption of work expressed by the Irishman. "Which, seeing's I reckon whoever owns that fool critter wouldn't've taken kind to having him killed out here, 'stead of all right 'n' proper in a slaughterhouse, I'm more'n obliged to you-all for cutting in so pronto and saving me from needing to do it."

"That's all right, Mr. Smith," claimed the tallest and oldest of the group, who had done the roping. His voice had the drawl of a Texan despite his Northern style of clothing, and it had the timbre of one long used to giving and having his orders accepted. "Except it wasn't going to any slaughterhouse, what the feller's bought it from us this morning said. They allowed they needed a mean ole mossy-horn bull for a Bill-Show they was figuring on running and concluded he'd be just what they wanted. Paid more than he'd've fetched on the hoof, so we got him penned on his lonesome for them to move when they was ready. Such's been done afore, so I didn't see nothing wrong with saying 'Why, sure, take him 'n' welcome.' "

"That being why they wanted him," Smith drawled sardonically, "they for sure didn't work overhard at keeping him safe penned. Fact being, was I asked, I'd say they turned him loose on purpose and made certain sure he'd be more'n just riled when he came out of the pen."

"Looked just a smidgin that ways to me," the self-appointed spokesman for the group of cowhands admitted. "Which being, I was wanting to ask those jaspers what the hell game they thought they were playing, but I saw Sam here'd likely need a mite of help, so we sort of drifted along to give it. Trouble being, when we were through, they'd lit out." Turning, he gazed in the direction taken by the trio in question and addressed his next words to the other cowhands. "Any of you boys know them?"

"They sure wasn't no kin of *mine!*" declared the Negro and, chuckling over his response, the rest of the cowhands denied all knowledge of the trio.

"We could sort of drift around and see could we cut their trail," the shortest and oldest of the group suggested in what appeared to be a hopeful fashion.

"And do it in all the bars you come across?" the tallest cowhand stated rather than merely guessed, his lazy drawl just as apparently exuding gratitude for the suggestion. "I reckon not, thank you 'most to death for offering. Go back to what you was doing and earn some of that money you're getting so well paid to do."

"Well," Smith said after all the cowhands except the Negro had left him with their spokesman. "Let's make us some *habla* now, shall we?"

"Lord, it's *bueno* to hear some good ole-fashioned Mex' talked, ain't it, Sam?" the remaining white cowhand declared, and received a nod of confirmation from the Negro. "Anyways, this here's Sam Wallace and I'm Tobe McKinley. Which, the formalities now having been done right 'n' proper, we'll take you to somebody's we conclude you'll be right pleased to meet."

Satisfied that he had met the person he was instructed to contact, the rusty-haired Texan accompanied the cowhands to an office used by railroad officials or others with business to carry out in the stockyards. Entering, he found himself confronted by a man considerably younger than he had expected. About an inch shorter than Smith and sturdily built, he was wearing good-quality range clothing originating from the same area as that worn by the cowhands. Despite having on spectacles and sporting a short, neatly trimmed reddish mustache that, taken with a mouthful of big teeth, tended to give his face a somewhat owlish look, he carried himself with easy assurance.

"Mr. Smith, meet Mr. Smith," McKinley introduced.

"By Godfrey, it's bully to make your acquaintance at last, Wax," the man to whom the rusty-haired Texan was being presented declared in a somewhat high-pitched and piping voice that failed to remove any trace of his masculinity. "I trust you'll forgive the lack of formality and will call me Teddy."

1. Why the cooperation was given is told in THE LAW OF THE GUN.
1a. A reciprocal cooperation that took place between Dusty Fog and Lieutenant Frank Ballinger—as he was then—of the Chicago Police Department is described in THE FORTUNE HUNTERS.
1b. Lieutenant Ballinger makes a guest appearance in THE REMITTANCE KID.
2. Information regarding Dusty Fog's career with the Texas Light Cavalry is given in Part Five, "A Time for Improvisation, Mr. Blaze," J. T.'s HUNDREDTH, *and several volumes of the Civil War series.*

15

THAT'S *MY* CAB

"Well, we're all ready to leave for Texas, or rather South Dakota if Samuel had been believed," remarked the man Waxahachie Smith had traveled so far and at considerable risk to meet. "I don't suppose those *hombres* who've been causing you so much trouble have lost the trail, do you?"

"I wouldn't want to have my life hang on it happening," the rusty-haired Texan replied, noticing that his companion seemed to show no anxiety over the possibility of forthcoming danger. "Unless I'm mistaken, the way the letter I got telling me where to meet you had been opened like it was never sealed or the envelope had been switched, that shifty-eyed jasper on the reception desk's been passing word about my doings ever since I hit town."

"Oh well, those little things are sent to try even the

best of us," Frank Smith said philosophically, still without showing any evidence of concern.

In the three days of their acquaintance, Wax had grown to like and respect the man who was helping him achieve his ambition to be able to return to and live in Texas without needing to fear arrest.[1]

Regardless of his physical appearance and flamboyant manner of speaking, Frank Smith struck the rusty-haired Texan as being very much a man, and one who could be counted upon in any emergency. What was more, despite being less than distinguished in appearance, he possessed a charisma that had gained the admiration of the cowhands who had helped save Wax from the bull in the stockyards and proved to have the same effect on several other equally tough and competent men with whom he came into contact. Even if Wax had not heard the subject mentioned by Tobias McKinley in Frank's temporary absence to answer the "call of nature," that he was unlikely to prove a liability and in need of protection should gunplay occur before their association ended was proved to the Texan's satisfaction.

Taking advantage of an offer to do so given by Chief of Detectives Frank Ballinger, the two Smiths had gone to the shooting range belonging to the Chicago Police Department. While there, Teddy—as he insisted upon being called—had proved an excellent shot with the Winchester Model of 1876 rifle he brought with his baggage. He also demonstrated skill at drawing and throwing lead accurately with the ivory-handled Colt Civilian Model Peacemaker he carried in a high-riding cross-draw holster on the broad waistbelt that he had also proved to have with his belongings. It was also apparent from various remarks he made that he was fully conversant with the cattle business and not just as it applied to the work he was chosen to carry out.

With one exception, nothing else of note had occurred during the remainder of the brief stay in Chicago. Having changed his cowhand clothing for Eastern attire, including a pair of Hersome gaiter boots to which he took grave exception and swore hurt in the way his regular high-heeled and sharp-toed footwear never did, Samuel Wallace had accompanied the two Smiths in the guise of general assistant to "Massa Teddy." He had reported after breakfast that morning that he had been approached by another Negro the previous evening and, after having supplied a couple of drinks, was asked whether he was going to be around for a big dice game to take place later in the week. Saying that he was disappointed at not being able to attend, on being prompted, he had said he was accompanying his boss on a special and secret mission to the South Dakotas before the appointed day. Asked when the departure would take place, he had said he did not know for sure but felt it would be fairly soon.

With all the arrangements made for traveling, including having some large wooden boxes labeled SURGICAL INSTRUMENTS, HANDLE WITH CARE in large red letters, but bearing no identifying name, dispatched by Wells Fargo to a ranch in South Dakota, the trio were gathered at the hotel ready to leave. As was to be expected in that day and age, Wallace was placed in charge of their baggage. In spite of the reason for Teddy going to Texas, this was nowhere near as bulky and impressive-looking as the items sent off as a decoy.

Going to the lobby to check out, the two Smiths fended off a request for a forwarding address—"in case any mail arrives after you are gone"—from the shifty-eyed desk clerk suspected by Wax of having opened the letter telling of the rendezvous with his namesake. Ignoring a suggestion that it was the policy of the establishment to acquire the required information, they had paid their respective bills. Then, acting as if they were confident that they had thrown any pursuers off their trail, they passed through the open double front door to where Wallace was waiting for them with a cabriolet of a size suitable for carrying the three of them and their baggage. It had been hired specially and not selected from the rank of smaller vehicles that plied for hire a short distance from the hotel's main entrance.

Giving the appearance of waiting for somebody while sitting in the lobby, a man dressed in garments suitable for the luxurious premises—albeit showing little sign of having received attention to keep them tidy—rose after the two Smiths walked by. He was about five feet nine in height, with a weedy build, less-than-tidy mousy longish brown hair, and pale dyspeptic features. Tossing aside the newspaper he had held, more as if wishing to keep his features concealed than to read its information, he rose and started to go after them. Before he had taken more than four steps, somebody collided with considerable violence against him. Not only did the unexpected impact cause him to stagger, but something thin and unyielding passed between his legs and tripped him so that he went sprawling to the floor.

"You clumsy, inconsiderate man. Why don't you look where you're going!"

Screeched in a somewhat tinny and definitely irate voice with a Southern accent and a suggestion of fairly advanced years, the words that followed the collision were uttered by a woman. She was about five feet seven in height, and the all-black clothing she had on conveyed the impression that she was somewhat dumpy in build. Because of the black veil suspended from below an otherwise undecorated hat of the same somber hue, nothing could be seen of her face. What was more, not only were the gloves she wore in keeping with the rest of her attire's resemblance to "widow's weeds," they prevented any indication of her marital status from being detected.

Like her victim, she had been making for the front

door after having sat reading—with muttered expressions of disgust at some of the contents—a magazine devoted to the activities of the more lighthearted members of Chicago's society. She, too, had discarded it and moved forward with surprising speed for one of her apparently no longer young age. What was more, because she gave the impression of trying to turn aside at the last minute, her right shoulder had rammed into his left arm with some force. The effect of the collision was compounded when the tightly furled black umbrella she carried passed between his legs, causing him to trip up.

Instead of waiting to find out whether her victim was hurt by the fall to the floor, having made her protest at the top of a still-powerful set of lungs, she resumed her intended departure at its earlier speed. On emerging from the hotel, if she was going anywhere except a short distance, it seemed she was in luck.

Having ignored requests for service by two potential passengers, although unoccupied and there having been no signal requesting such an action from the doorman dressed somewhat unconvincingly—as his ruddy features were much more Irish in lines than Gallic—after the fashion of a French Zouave soldier who regularly performed such a function for guests, the driver of a vehicle designed along the lines of a British dog cart and drawn by a good-looking horse had moved forward from the foremost position on the rank and was coming to a halt outside the building.

Tall, bulky in a flabby way rather than suggestive of firm flesh beneath cheap clothing little different from that worn by others in his line of work, the driver looked to be in his mid-twenties. There was a pasty pallor about his heavily jowled porcine face that seemed strange for one whose occupation ought to have exposed it to tanning by the elements. Not only had he displayed a surprising lack of interest in earning money by picking up passengers, but his handling of the horse was much less competent than might have been expected from one who plied for hire in an affluent part of the city.

"Take me to the—!" the elderly-looking woman began, waving her umbrella to emphasize the words.

"I'm already tak—!" the driver commenced, his voice lacking any suggestion of the masculine roughness so often characteristic of his kind, but he, too, was not permitted to complete his statement.

"Of course you aren't!" the woman asserted. "You've nobody in the back."

"That's *my* cab!" yelped the man who had suffered the collision in the lobby, having regained his feet and hurried on to the sidewalk.

"Nonsense!" the cause of the mishap veritably snorted in what appeared to be righteous indignation. "I was here first, not you!"

"But I'd order—!" the man began, his voice even more squeaky than it previously sounded.

"How could you when I was out here *first?*" the woman demanded. Then, glancing away, she gave a grunt redolent of satisfaction at something she had seen and raised her voice in a stridently commanding yell of "Officer!"

"Yes, ma'am?" asked the patrolman of the Chicago Police Department who had been farther along the street but came striding forward in answer to the summons. His accent was Irish, as would have been the case with the majority of officers in his organization. "Was there something up?"

"There was and still is," the woman confirmed. "This person is trying to make out he has the *right* to take the cabriolet I need to use."

"But I ordered it—!" the man said in what sounded like a gobble.

"Don't talk *rubbish!*" the woman interrupted. "You've never come outside for at least half an hour, as I know well. And you didn't send to ask the doorman to do it for you."

"Is that the rights of it, sir?" the patrolman asked after a glance toward the doorkeeper, who—having no desire to be caught in the middle of an argument between two people who had emerged from the hotel—turned away and appeared to be concentrating on what was happening in the opposite direction.

"Of course it is!" the woman insisted before the man could speak. "And I expect *you* to do something to see I get my rightly dues, Officer. The chief of police is a personal friend of mine."

"Well now, sir," the patrolman said, directing a look that was redolent of an unexpressed *There's nothing else I can do, seeing's who she is* toward the pallid-faced victim of the collision. "Don't you reckon's how it'd be the gentlemanly thing to do to be letting the lady have this cab? I can right easy get you another from the rank down there."

"I—I—!" the young man started. Having stared for a moment along the street in the opposite direction to that indicated by the officer, as the driver of the cabriolet was doing with an equal intensity, he let out a hiss of annoyance. Then he gave a shrug and went on in a bitter tone, "Oh well, she may as well have it."

"I don't want it now," the woman declared with a toss of her head and another wave of her umbrella, which this time suggested derision. "Taking it would be like I was beholden to him, and that I wouldn't want to be!"

"Wha—?" croaked the man, but stopped as if words had failed him.

Paying no attention to any of the other principal participants in the scene she had provoked, the woman stalked back into the hotel without deigning to say another word. Although her victim and the driver seemed close to apoplexy, the patrolman gave a shrug as if he had expected nothing else from her. Then, also without speaking, he resumed his beat in a manner suggesting that he thought he had done all he could under the circumstances.

"Where are *they?*" the pallid-faced man demanded angrily after the officer had passed beyond hearing distance.

"How would I know?" the driver snarled, his tone taking on the timbre of one better educated than might be expected for somebody in such a line of work. "They turned off the street while I was talking to that old bitch."

"Going the way they set off, they must be headed for the railroad depot," the man asserted with the air of one drawing an indisputable conclusion. "Let's get there. If that nigger of yours got the right of it and they're heading for South Dakota, they'll have to take a westbound train. So we'll be able to make sure they're aboard and, and when we're sure, we can leave it to somebody else to see what can be done about it."

"How'd everything go?" Chief of Detectives Frank Ballinger asked as the woman wearing widow's weeds entered a luxurious suite of rooms on the second floor of the hotel.

"Couldn't have gone smoother" was the reply, but the voice had a tone that was very different from the one it had had while the woman was downstairs and outside the building.

While making the assertion, after letting fall her umbrella, the woman reached up to slip free the black veil and removed it along with the black hat. Doing so brought into view neatly coiffured black hair just grizzled with a hint of gray, a head that seemed too trim for her bulky-looking frame, and a face that had a mature beauty in addition to showing strength of will and intelligence beyond average in its lines. Tossing the headdress onto the writing table by the door, she unbuttoned the front of her outer attire, taking no notice of the tall and craggily good-looking police officer's presence. However, its removal provided yet another surprise. What came into view was a willowy, yet far from flat-chested, body clad in a masculine black shirt, with matching skintight riding breeches ending in Wellington leg boots also suited for equestrian wear.

"By the Lord, Belle," Ballinger said as the padded outer garment that had supplied the suggestion of bulk was taken off by its wearer to be placed on the bed. "Seeing you in one of your disguises takes me back a spell."[2]

"Longer than either of us wants to consider, I'll wager," Belle Boyd replied with a wry smile; her voice was still that of a Southron, albeit less strident and younger-sounding than previously. She flexed her arms and twisted her torso for a moment, then continued, "I tell you, Frank, I'd just about forgotten how much fun and satisfaction playing a game like I just did could be since the boss told me I deserved to be assigned to training at headquarters. We both knew he meant he thought I was getting too old to play the Rebel Spy anymore."

"If you're too old, I'd hate to have come up against you when you was young and limber," the chief asserted.

"Flatterer!" Belle drawled. "But don't stop doing it, please. By the way, can you give a special word of thanks to that patrolman? He showed up just as you promised he would and helped me quite a bit."

"I'll tell him, seeing as how it's a fair time since he got into the blue and walked a beat," Ballinger promised. "He's one of my sharpest detective sergeants. Anyways, how do you reckon everything went?"

"Like was needed," Belle assessed. "Galloway and Malan took the bait like a hungry bigmouth bass rising for a bullfrog, although neither of them is as good-looking or useful most times. They've lost Wax and Teddy and will waste some more time and money if they act upon what Sam Wallace told their man about our boys heading for South Dakota. Yes, taking all I've been told by Wax and seen since he got here, I'd say *everything* is going just the way it was planned."

"We didn't see them *anywhere* when we finally got to the railroad depot," George Galloway said petulantly, his dyspeptic face working with anger. "The westbound had left and nobody we asked could remember whether they'd gone with it or not."

"Sylvester said that he was told they were going to South Dakota," Hugo Malan put in sullenly, realizing that the other was trying to lay all the blame upon him for the debacle that afternoon. He was a painter who rarely if ever found anybody willing to purchase even one of his works, not a driver, so he resented the implication that his lack of skill along that line had delayed the arrival at the depot, even though it was true. "So they'd *have* to take the westbound."

"A less than amicable discussion was taking place in the dining room of the mansion owned by Malcolm Penny in the wealthiest district of Chicago. The oldest and richest of the group, he believed the amount of his own and other of his dupes' money he had already expended upon the business under debate gave him the right to serve as its spokesman.

For all his affluence, motivated as were most of his kind, by a desire to retain his wealth if they should ever gain enough power to take over the country and implement their policies, Penny was a longtime supporter of the most radical elements in the Republican Party, and the men who had gathered shared his political outlook. It was they, along with others of their kind in Texas and Washington, D.C., who were behind the attempts to prevent a solution from being found for the problems

caused by the mysterious disease afflicting the cattle and
threatening the economy of the Lone Star State. What
amounted to a council of war was taking place, but as
yet nothing had been said that suggested a way out of
the dilemma.

However, the repeated failures to take effective measures against the man credited with being able to produce a cure for the Texas fever and possessing the
knowledge to bring this about were getting ever more
annoying. Not the least cause of animosity was the
amount of money that had been expended upon the
ventures toward that end that failed to produce any required result. Being mean in financial matters as well as
in spirit, all of them bitterly resented the loss of so much
money without anything to show for it.

"Why the hell would they go to South Dakota when
Smith had been sent for to find a cure for the Texas
fever?" Penny demanded, but he did not wait for an
answer since there was something to be raised he considered more important. "Anyway, they've gone, and
what was tried here was no more successful than in
Texas."

"It didn't run to as much money," pointed out Paul
Magee, a lawyer who—like most of the others—relied
upon money from his middle class–middle management
family to cover an invariably inept performance of his
duties. Being the one responsible for the abortive attempt to kill Waxahachie Smith at the stockyards, he
sought to change the subject. "That damned Welshman
in Texas keeps writing to ask for the twenty-five hundred
dollars Steffen made him hand over for expenses."

"Steffen's been the biggest expense—and failure—of
all," Penny growled.

"I can't see why we didn't use somebody of our own
instead of taking on a hired killer," Magee went on,
hoping nobody remembered that it was at his suggestion
the choice was made.

"Because none of you, or anybody else, would do it," Penny reminded.

"I was told that he and the feller who's hard of hearing he works with are the best at it," Magee stated sulkily, his tenuous connections with the criminal elements of the city having produced the information.

"Didn't you ever meet either of them face-to-face?" Malan challenged.

"I met Steffen," Denzil Kline claimed in the high-pitched voice that, along with his somewhat effeminate bearing, had caused him to be close to a failure in his career in the theater.

"What does he look like?" Magee asked, having heard that the man in question tried to avoid making personal contact.

"Tall, thickset, with longish black hair," the inept actor replied. "His face was pallid and he had a very large bulbous nose and big walrus mustache. I didn't see his eyes because he was wearing dark-lens glasses."

"A man looking like that would stand out in any crowd," Magee opined, unaware that Dusty Fog might have found the description of interest. "Provided that's what he really looks like. I've heard they call him Walt the Actor because he was one and is real good at disguising himself."

"You said something about him working with a man who's hard of hearing," Galloway put in, more from a desire to keep the conversation away from the abortive part he and Malan had played in the events of that afternoon. "Why would he do that?"

"To pick up information," the less-than-successful lawyer explained. "The feller can lip-read and learn things from a distance that it would be impossible to overhear."

At that moment, Penny's butler entered carrying a buff-colored envelope on a silver tray. After the man had withdrawn, the rest of the group watched in silence as their host removed a similarly colored sheet of paper from the envelope and studied what was printed on it.

"This is from Steffen, in the usual code," Penny announced. "What it comes down to is that he claims he's discovered where Smith will be working in Texas—!"

"That's *good!*" Malan enthused.

"Wait until I've finished, damn you!" Penny snarled. "He says he wants five thousand dollars sent to him before he'll do anything about it—and from what Paul's told me about him, unless he gets it, he'll tell all he knows to those damned Texans who're behind having Smith go there."

Unbeknownst to the group of conspirators, everything they were saying was being eavesdropped upon.

Wearing the appropriate attire and with sufficient changes by a skill at disguise that had served her well all through her career, Belle Boyd had acquired the post as housemaid for Penny on first receiving a hint of what was in the wind. Having reported for her duties after helping deal with Galloway and Malan, she was now using her old trick of listening through the wall of the room next to where the meeting was taking place. She considered what she had heard to be worth the risks she was taking to listen.

1. *Although we have used Waxahachie Smith's surname when referring to him so far in this narrative, to avoid confusion between them, we will be calling him "Wax" and his companion "Frank," unless employing the requested name "Teddy."*
2. *An earlier meeting between Belle "the Rebel Spy" Boyd and Lieutenant Frank Ballinger—as he was at the time—is recorded in* THE REMITTANCE KID.
3. *Details pertaining to the career of Belle Boyd as a secret service agent for the Confederate States during the War Between the States—hence her sobriquet, "the Rebel Spy"—and the United States when it ended are given in various volumes of the Civil War and Floating Outfit series.*

16

I MIGHT'VE KNOWN
IT'D BE *HIM*

"Well, I'll be switched," Waxahachie Smith said in a voice that came close to rapture as he gazed at the small ranch house he and his two companions were approaching. "The ole place looks as good as it always did, but I'm damned if I can remember those grassy mounds scattered around it."

"They do say the moles in Texas grow to the same prodigious dimensions as everything else," Frank Smith remarked with a smile provoked by the show of feelings from the generally unemotional rusty-haired man with whom he was coming toward their destination. "And, if that is the cause, I want to shoot some of them for my trophy room."

"Just one of 'em'd make a dandy coat once its hide was skinned out 'n' dressed," Samuel Wallace declared from where he was driving a small wagon, once more dressed in his cowhand's clothes. "Only, I'd bet that same one'd be plumb hell on wheels to stop should he set it in mind to charge."

Given the interference and confusion that had been produced by the efforts of Belle Boyd, although they and Wallace had followed the same route taken on the outward journey by Wax, the trip from Chicago had passed without any further attempts being made by the men who were trying to prevent a cure for the Texas fever. Even before the trio reached Arkansas, the Negro had traveled among his own kind. Before leaving Chicago, he had stated that his presence would be more credible if he did so. What was more, he could have a better opportunity of gathering information while with members of his own race. While he learned nothing of importance, he conceded later, there had been a personal benefit from his decision. On several occasions, he had been invited to be taught how to shoot dice, and being something of an expert at this activity, had picked up a reasonable amount of money.

The only incident of note along the way had occurred shortly after the trio had arrived at Little Rock. Primed by hard liquor, a loafer in a bar they visited had been sufficiently misled by the appearance presented by Teddy as to call him "Four-Eyes" and demand that he buy drinks for the house. Removing and handing his spectacles to Wax, the seemingly harmless intended victim proved to be just as competent at handling his fists and employing roughhouse brawling tactics as he had already been when handling his firearms on the range belonging to the Chicago Police Department.

As there was no railroad going in the required direction after Little Rock, Wax and Teddy had continued their journey on horseback, the latter proving himself equally adept at riding. Still in his pose as assistant to "Doctor Smith," Wallace drove the wagon that had been waiting for them and carried their personal belongings as well as equipment intended for the forth-coming work.

They crossed the Red River a few miles south of Tex-arkana, avoiding the town as being the most likely choice for anybody who might be on the lookout for the return of his party should—as was likely to have hap-pened—the pretense of going from Chicago to South Dakota have been discovered to be false by their ene-mies, which they all conceded was likely to have hap-pened. Wax had been hard put to conceal the pleasure he was feeling at having finally arrived back in Texas after the enforced absence caused by the legal complica-tions that had arisen after the way he exacted a well-deserved revenge upon the Fuentes brothers. Both his companions had guessed at the depth of his feelings and were amused by observing how he tried to prevent them from showing.

On entering Texas, the route chosen by Wax kept the trio clear of the one by which he had traveled on his journey to Chicago. Because the wagon was carrying enough supplies for them to have no need to go in search of a meal or other provisions, they had kept clear of towns and even other human habitations as far as was possible. The way they were now dressed had not been such as to attract attention to them on the few occasions when they had had chance and unavoidable contact with other human beings. Although the attire worn by two of them was that of a cowhand from a northern cattle-raising state, there was nothing else to make them suffi-ciently conspicuous to invite curiosity.

With the restrictions posed by the journey until reach-ing the Red River at an end, Frank Smith now wore his gunbelt and Colt Civilian Model Peacemaker, and his Winchester Model of 1876 Centennial rifle was in the boot of the double-girthed Texas saddle that Wax had procured for his use along with a couple of excellent horses. With regard to the saddle, on several occasions

he had stated in typical range-country fashion that he
hoped none of his friends from back home would ever
hear he had used it instead of his vastly superior
Meanea Cheyenne roll rig. Despite his looks and flamboyant way of speaking, he had proved to be a good
cook and the possessor of other accomplishments indicative of a very good knowledge of living under the conditions they now faced.

As a precaution, the trio had gone into the seat of
Titus County, thus breaking the habit of avoiding other
human beings. While at Mount Pleasant, Wax had visited the sheriff to present the "proof" that he was "Aloysius W. Ramsbottom the Third." The documentary
"evidence" had been accepted without question by the
peace officer, but he had commented that there was no
need for further concern on the matter of possible mistaken identity, because the state attorney general had
recently sent notification to all law-enforcement agen-
cies that the warrant for Waxahachie Smith was being
held in temporary abeyance pending an inquiry into
whether the reason for its issue could be classed as having passed the statute of limitations. He also claimed
that certain very prominent citizens whose wishes were
likely to be respected and acted upon—particularly
those residing in Rio Hondo County—had passed the
word that anybody trying to arrest Wax regardless of the
information would answer to them for doing so.

In spite of the reduced need to exercise extra vigi-
lance on account of the warrant having been temporar-
ily lifted, the trio did not allow themselves to become
complacent and unwary. Nevertheless, although Teddy
and Wallace had claimed to having felt they were being
kept under observation since leaving Mount Pleasant,
none of them had been able to detect any sign of the
watcher. Certainly, if there was somebody dogging their
trail for some reason, nothing happened to make them
assume that this was for some hostile purpose. What

was more, when they were about a day's journey from their destination of the rusty-haired Texan's ranch in Ellis County—his sobriquet had arisen from his frequent references to having been born at its seat, Waxahachie—they had decided the undetected scrutiny was no longer taking place.

Watching the woman and four men who came from the ranch house, Wax felt some qualms. However, they were not caused by wondering if the woman and men might be in the pay of his enemies. Despite the long period he had been away—he realized the redbone coonhound that had given notice of the approach of his party must be a descendant of the one so highly prized by everybody at the place prior to his departure—he recognized all of them. Helped by their sons, Cy Junior and Waldo, Martha and Cyrus Lombard had kept the spread going in his absence. Furthermore, going by what he had seen while crossing the range he owned, they had done so in an exemplary fashion. Because of that, he wondered how they might be reacting to his return and being at liberty to take up permanent residence on the property which they had every right to regard as their home.

All of Wax's qualms vanished when he saw the warm and friendly manner being displayed by all of the family as he brought his horses to a halt in front of them. Showing a not unexpected tact, Teddy and Wallace had halted a short distance away and were watching what was happening with a well-concealed interest. As the rusty-haired Texan swung from his saddle, the Lombards moved forward, exuding a welcome that he found most comforting.

"It's *good* to see you home at last, Waldo," greeted Martha, as plump and pleasantly homely as Wax remembered her from the old days, as she advanced with arms outstretched to embrace him.

"It sure is," confirmed Cyrus, who looked the typical

old Texas cowhand he had always been, offering a work-hardened hand to be shaken.

"You won't get no argument from us'n's on *that*," Cy Junior asserted with an equal warmth, and his younger brother—whose appearances still gave Wax the impression of being their father at different stages of his youth—proffered a similar sentiment. "We can sure use somebody around to help with the chores."

Before any more could be said, Martha insisted that Wax and his companions go into the house to rest up and take some decent food after their long journey. Nor, except for permitting the necessary introductions to be performed, would she allow any conversation until she had carried out her desire to see the trio fed in the fashion for which Wax retained fond memories.

"Reckon they's still after you, boy?" Cyrus inquired after the rusty-haired Texan had told what had happened since his return in response to the summons received from Dusty Fog.

"I wouldn't want to count on 'em quitting just 'cause we throwed 'em off our trail some in Chicago," Wax warned, then turned his gaze to the elderly woman. "Which being, Martha, it might be as well for you to go spend a few days with your kinfolks in town."

"The Comanches couldn't make me do that," the woman answered in a spirited fashion that drew grins from all her audience, even the one who had made the suggestion. "Which being, this place's even better fixed now than it was when those red varmints were on the rampage."

After the comment was made, Wax paid greater attention than he had so far to his surroundings. Built when there was a need for a structure sturdy enough to ward off attacks by hostile Indians, the house gave no indication of having deteriorated to any noticeable extent. In fact, he noticed for the first time that some improvements had been newly made. The walls had al-

ways been thick enough to hold out bullets as well as
arrows, but the thinner planks forming the loopholed
shutters at the windows had a lining of sheet iron that
had only recently been installed.

Considering the possiblity of an attack should their
presence be discovered by their enemies, Wax was in
favor of the modifications. However, he still had misgivings over the grassy mounds around the buildings, which
he did not remember being there when he left home to
become a Texas ranger. Nor was his apprehension lessened when Cyrus admitted that there had been a few
occasions in the past few days when strangers, whom
Martha assessed as being hard cases of a kind she would
not want her sons to know, had called requesting a meal
while passing through on the way to some undisclosed
destination and purpose. He was given a further cause
for concern by Cy's remark that one of the sheriff's deputies had dropped by a couple of days back and mentioned there were several more of the same kind in
Waxahachie for some unexplained reason.

Taking everything into account, Wax considered that
he would be easier in his mind if the mounds did not
offer such well-placed cover for anybody wanting to attack the house.

The attack was launched shortly after midnight on the
evening that Waxahachie Smith returned to his home.

With the trio settled in to Martha Lombard's satisfaction, the rest of the day had passed enjoyably and without incident. She had insisted on hearing about Wax's
activities and received a short account of the more hu-
morous incidents up to his long-awaited return to his
home state. There had been some discussion on the
problem of finding a cure for the Texas fever, with Frank
Smith asserting his belief that this could be achieved as
a result of his involvement. When Wax had raised the
matter of the mounds, he was told they had just seemed

to grow, and Cyrus and his sons, all sharing the typical cowhand aversion to riding the blister end of a shovel, had decided against trying to level them.

Because of the news about there being some hard cases assembled in Waxahachie, the rusty-haired Texan had insisted that a guard be maintained even though there would be a full moon and the redbone coonhound could be counted on to detect any unwanted callers in good time for defensive preparations to be made. He and Cyrus were sharing the duty, spending the time in a sotto voce discussion about the future—which he had stated would be to everybody's satisfaction—when the dog justified the confidence in its abilities by coming to its feet and giving a low growl as it went to stand by the closed front door. Looking through the loophole in the right-side window, while the elderly man was waking the other occupants of the house, Wax saw three masculine figures carrying rifles advancing on foot and, as Cy had said the deputy put the number of hard cases in Waxahachie at fifteen to twenty, felt sure more were approaching from the other sides.

Responding with a speed indicating that such a summons was not being received for the first time—Teddy giving the same impression as the Texans and the Negro—none of them having done more than removed their footwear before retiring, all the remaining occupants of the house were quickly assembled. They went to the positions they had been allocated when the arrangements for coping with such a situation were made earlier in the evening.

"Who-all's out there?" Cyrus called after he was notified that the defensive preparations were completed.

Although the three men within Wax's range of vision were probably surprised by the discovery that their presence had been detected, as were the rest around the building if various sounds were any guide, they reacted with a speed that suggested they were not engaged upon such an activity for the first time. Just as the rusty-haired Texan had surmised would prove the case, they took cover behind two of the mounds that had caused him so many misgivings. Not that he was surprised by this. If the visitors had been scouting the lay of the land in preparation for such an attack, they would not have failed to notice such effective positions and the protection they offered from the guns of the defenders. Nor was he alone in his assessment of the situation.

"I say there, Wax!" Teddy called from the bedroom assigned as his defensive position, still employing his somewhat pompous manner of speech despite the situation. "These fellers of mine are taking cover behind the molehills you've got such a dislike for."

"So's my bunch, Massa Wax!" Wallace announced as he studied the situation from his position in the kitchen.

"So why'n't you start shooting at 'em?" Cyrus suggested, and sounds indicative of amusement arose from his sons. "Big as they be, Texas moles don't make's stout 'n' sturdy hills's some folks reckon."

With the suggestion made, the elderly man lined his Spencer rifle and squeezed the trigger. Far from being new, its kind had first been manufactured in 1860—although the one he was holding was one of the improved Model 1865. The result of the shot was as much of a surprise to Wax as to the man at whom it was aimed. On striking the grassy surface, the .56-caliber bullet passed through the mound with surprisingly little resistance. His hat having been ripped from his head by the lead, the hard case let out a yell of alarm and rose instinctively from what he had thought would be an ideal shelter from any gunfire directed his way.

Giving a derisive cackle, Cyrus operated the trigger guard–cum–lever to eject the spent cartridge case and place the next of the six rounds in the tubular magazine. However, swiftly as he moved, by the time he had carried out the necessary manual cocking of the hammer—

a feature that prevented the Spencer from enjoying the popularity attained by the Henry and its successors in the Winchester range of rifles equipped with a mechanism that obviated the need to carry out the second action—the man had dropped once more behind the mound.

"You Smiths never was worth a cuss at doing, young Wax," Cyrus stated while realigning the Spencer. "Or are you maybe waiting to get asked all perlite-like to get her done, if you wants to cut in on this folderol?"

Despite being amazed by the unexpected and seemingly inexplicable turn of events, the rusty-haired Texan responded to the question by aiming the Lightning rifle—selected as being better suited than the slip gun to his present needs—at the man who was doing the same with a Winchester from the left side of the second mound, and who presented a marginally easier target than the one to the right, since Wax's weapon was at his off-side shoulder. Wondering whether the result attained by Cyrus was some kind of fluke, despite something of the sort clearly having been expected, he made a slight adjustment to the alignment and touched off a shot. Although only .44 in caliber, as opposed to the larger size of the Spencer's lead, the bullet he discharged passed through the mound and elicited a response more serious in effect than the one he had just seen caused. A great howl was heard and the Winchester's barrel tilted into the air before it fell from its owner's grasp as a result of the pain caused by the flat-nosed bullet plowing into his left shoulder.

Manipulating the trombone slide mechanism that served to differentiate the Colt Lightning from its Winchester contemporaries and changing his point of aim, despite still being unable to fathom what was producing the surprising results, Wax sent the next round at the mound rather than the second of the men sheltering behind it. He achieved another hit, this time producing

an even more dramatic effect. Lurching upward with
blood flowing from the hole in his chest and dropping
his rifle, the second attacker toppled sideways to measure his length on the ground.

If the sounds that arose from the other sides of the
building were any indication, Wax decided the rest of
the defenders were attaining similar successes to those
of Cyrus and himself. Following the shots from inside
the building, there were cries of pain and yells of alarm
all around. Then, demoralized by the unexpected turn
of events, those of the would-be attackers able to do so
turned and hurried off in the directions from which they
had come.

"Looks like they didn't take kind' to them Texas
molehills," Cyrus remarked as the sounds of the hurried
departure faded away. "Somehow, way they was
throwed up, I had me a sneaky suspicion's such could
prove the case."

"Was that some of *your* doing?" Wax inquired, deducing from the way the last part of the comment was
worded that the mounds were not made naturally.

"Waal, much's I'd like to give you a 'yes' to that," the
elderly man replied, "I can't come out all truthful truly
true 'n' say it was, but I reckon you'll be meeting the
gent who come up with the notion 'n' fixed for it to be
carried out soon's he's seen those jaspers ain't fixing to
come back again tonight."

"I might've known it'd be *him*," Wax declared. "Let's
go take a look at those *hombres* who're still around."

An examination—performed with precautions taken
against the possibility of reprisals being attempted—informed the defenders that there was no fear of such an
eventuality. Although the man affected by a shoulder
wound made good his escape, as did a couple more injured in a similar fashion—more by accident than delib-
erate intent—by Waldo and Teddy, Wax's second victim
and one who was hit by Wallace were dead. Another,

who had been lying in front of where Cy was positioned, had sustained a serious wound that, in the absence of more highly skilled attention than Martha was capable of producing for all her experience in dealing with injuries of various kinds, caused his death before much time had elapsed.

Shortly after the examination of the area around the cabin was started, a flurry of rifle shots sounded in the direction taken by the fleeing attackers. When these ended, there sounded a savage whoop of a kind not heard for many years in the vicinity of Waxahachie. Teddy and Wallace reached for their weapons, but apart from Cyrus remarking, "It's *him* and he's all right!" none of the others paid any attention to it.

The elderly woman was just rejoining the men in the dining room to announce that the wounded attacker had died, without saying more than to give his name and the address of his parents—to which he wanted news of his fate to be sent—when the redbone gave another warning of somebody approaching. However, even if a yell of "Hey, Wax and the rest of you, don't shoot, it's only *me!*" had not been heard, the way in which the rider was coming without attempting to keep his presence unsuspected would have prevented anybody from feeling concern.

Coming through the door on being given permission, removing his low-crowned and wide-brimmed Texas-style J. B. Stetson hat as he did so, the newcomer proved to be a tall man clad from head to foot in black clothing. There was just a hint of graying in his coal-black hair and a few lines on his Indian-dark face, which would have given a suggestion of close to babyish innocence had it not been for his feral-looking red-hazel eyes. Only the dark brown walnut grips of an old Colt Model of 1848 Dragoon revolver, butt forward for a low cavalry twist-hand draw in the holster of his gunbelt, and the ivory handle of a massive bowie knife sheathed at the left differed from the somber hue of his garb.

"Sounds like you had a mite of fuss back a whiles, Lon," Wax remarked.

"Not as much as *they* did," replied the Ysabel Kid, who was continuing the part he had been assigned to play in the attempt to have a cure found for the Texas fever. "I was ready to let you know they was coming, only it wasn't needed and I soon saw you was handing those yahoos their asking-fors without needing me to cut in. So I snuck along after them when they lit a shuck. Then damn me if they didn't stop after 'round a mile and one of 'em starts saying's how they should come back to finish what they was sent to do and some of the others seemed of a like mind. I recognized him as a loudmouthed yack who didn't want to take the warning from the ole moccasin I left in their camp afore I snuck off with their hosses one night when you was headed for Chicago, Wax. So I concluded, him being a mite too trigger fast and up from Texas for my liking, he'd have to be showed what it meant."

"That would be what all the shooting was about, then," Teddy guessed.

"Why, sure," the Kid agreed. "Seems like he wasn't took with the notion when I yelled for them to get moving or else, and they went for else. Some of the other knobheads figured to help him, but sort of had trouble working out where I was until I started cutting loose, which sort of discouraged them, 'specially after I'd put down the loudmouth and two more. So they went on their way, and from what I heard being said, I concluded they aren't figuring on coming back, nor doing nothing else save getting their gear, then getting as much distance as they can from Waxahachie. So I might as well head along here to see if there was any chance of a cup of coffee."

"I'll fetch you one, Lon," Martha promised, having

left a pot on the stove to be used by the man standing watch.

"I tell you-all one thing," the Kid drawled as the woman was making for the kitchen. "I'm not sorry this chore is just about through. Like Rainey said when she heard what I was told to do, I'm getting too old for the amount of sage-henning, with ole Mother Earth for a mattress and the stars as a roof, that I've been having to do most of the time while Dusty and Mark was able to lie all warm and comfortable in their beds comes night."[1]

1. *How the Ysabel Kid met Rainey Smith, who later became his wife, is told in* GUNS IN NIGHT.

17

WE WERE ON TO YOU RIGHT FROM THE START

Walking down the stairs of the Gunnison Hotel shortly after ten o'clock in the morning, meaning to have his bags taken to the stage depot so he could shake the dust of Texas from his heels as soon as possible, Walter "the Actor" Steffen did not feel the slightest concern when he saw that two men were standing in the entrance hall. One was Waxahachie Smith and the other was a somewhat insignificant-looking bespectacled man wearing what—had Steffen been better acquainted with such matters—he would have known was the attire of a cowhand from a more northern cattle-raising state.

Having complete faith in the disguise he had selected for use while bringing what he hoped would be the conclusion of what had so far proven an unsatisfactory, albeit not unprofitable, affair to its conclusion, the Actor felt sure that the rusty-haired Texan would not recognize him as the "gambler" met in Hereford.[1] Except that he had on a shorter black wig, the rest of the amendments he had made to his appearance were those he had worn in Austin and, unbeknownst to him, Denzil Kline had described to the other liberals in Chicago. Furthermore, he now had on the garb and other accoutrements of priest of the Catholic Church who served in an Eastern city.

Of course, selecting such attire precluded Steffen from wearing the gunbelt and Colt Peacemaker that he had used to kill Joel Daly for trying to trick him into believing the first attempt to gun down Waxahachie Smith had met with success, and that formed part of his "costume"—he always thought in theatrical terms for everything employed in his disguises—when he appeared as a professional gambler at Hereford. However, he had a short-barreled Merwin & Hulbert Army Pocket revolver in a spring-retention shoulder holster beneath the left side of his jacket, and because he carried this more frequently than the Colt while working, as he had always done before in the East, he considered himself to be even better with it. What was more, as had always been the case back East, he was convinced its presence would not be suspected unless the need arose to bring it into rapid use.

Taking everything into consideration, the Actor judged that the time spent in Texas had proved unsuccessful even though there had been some—if not as much as he had hoped—money to show for the expenditure in time and effort put into carrying out the plan for which he was hired. Never one to accept blame, he attributed the repeated failures to having to rely on assistance from others besides his regular partner. In fact, he thought that the only positive parts of the affair had come about through his and Amos Cruikshank's efforts. Not that even these, apart from having claimed the offered bounty for bringing about the death of Edmund Dell in Austin, had amounted to much.

The main problem for Steffen had been that his only contact in Texas proved to be far less useful than he had been led to assume was the case. Therefore, the information he had received, taken with the low price he had offered in return for services rendered—mistakenly believing that nothing higher would be expected by the dull-witted denizens of the West he had expected to meet—had enabled him to obtain assistance of only a low quality. With the exception of an old-timer who had given support after some incident during the pursuit of Smith from Hereford, none of the men he hired had shown any signs of intelligence or initiative. Or, if it was the latter, whatever was done ended badly.

Added to snippets of information gathered mainly as a result of Cruikshank's ability to read lips, a chance meeting with a drunken cowhand in Fort Worth while collecting the reward for Dell had supplied the place to which the two Smiths would go after having made the successful escape from Chicago. Receiving the money Steffen had demanded from Malcolm Penny, they had hired assistance—including some of the men used in the abortive pursuit of the rusty-haired Texan—and made a rendezvous at Waxahachie.

Only one of the men who had been sent to kill the two Smiths at the ranch where the Actor had learned they would be staying returned to notify him of the failure to do so. He said all the survivors had not waited until morning before taking what he called a greaser standoff, and he meant to follow their example now that he had fulfilled what he considered to be his obligations by delivering the news. Having no desire to attempt flight on horseback, or to try to hire a buckboard in which to do so, Steffen and Cruikshank had elected to leave by the eastbound stagecoach when it arrived. Only the man who had brought the news knew either of them, and they felt sure he would not be available for questioning. Therefore, should any of the bunch who were unable to leave the ranch have been taken alive, there was no way Smith could learn where to find them.

Swinging his gaze from the two men, the Actor caught the eye of his partner and gave a quick nod in their direction.

On the point of emerging from the dining room where he had just finished a leisurely breakfast, Cruikshank came to an immediate halt when he saw the reason for the Actor's signal. However, he too saw little cause for alarm. Like Steffen, particularly since he no longer had on the false beard and wig worn in Hereford, he bore little resemblance to his persona while playing the role of a professor of mathematics. His attire was more suitable for the moderately successful representative of an Eastern mail-order company he was purporting to be. Therefore, he had no doubt that he would be an unsuspected factor should he have guessed wrong and his companion needed support to carry out the assignment for which they had been hired. With that in mind, hiding his ear trumpet behind his back, he put his right hand into the front of his jacket where he was armed in the same way as his partner.

"Why, howdy, Mr. Sidcup," Waxahachie Smith greeted, coming to a halt facing the black-dressed man in the attire of a Catholic priest. "Or should I say 'Howdy, Actor Steffen'?"

"I don't know what you mean, my son," the hired killer stated, needing only a moment to recover from the shock caused by what he had heard.

"The hell you *don't*," the rusty-haired Texan declared. "It's no use trying to pull a bluff, *hombre*. We were on to you right from the start."

When making the statement, Wax was speaking the truth.

On learning what was being planned by liberals imbued with the close to paranoid hatred their kind always felt for everybody who declined to follow exactly the dictates of their will—and some having a financial stake that made them just as eager to try to ruin the cattle business in the Lone Star State by means of playing upon fears of the so-called Texas fever—Belle Boyd had been determined to thwart them. Notifying Dusty Fog of all she had discovered, she had offered to keep supplying all the pertinent information to come her way. She had also been confident that the small Texan would take adequate measures to circumvent the scheme at his end.

Justifying the confidence of the Rebel Spy, Dusty, with the full support of his wife, had set about making preparations to deal with the situation. When laying their plans, Freddie and he had seen a way they might also help Wax circumvent the problem of the warrant still open against him if he returned to his home state. Being immediately promised the willing support of Mark Counter and the Ysabel Kid, they had set the scheme in motion.

One of the items of information Belle had sent was that a notorious Eastern hired killer—noted for his ability at adopting a variety of excellently produced disguises—and his partner had been selected by liberals in Chicago to use whatever means might be required to make sure a cure for the Texas fever was not discovered. The Rebel Spy also claimed that the men would be commencing their task by seeking information in Austin and that they had been told there was somebody in the service of Governor Matthew Anderson—whose name she had not learned—who would be able to help them learn much of what they needed to know. Being suspicious where what she called "civil servants" espousing "liberal" pretensions were concerned, it was at Freddie's instigation that they made use of Edmund Dell to make sure that such news of their activities as they wanted known reached the conspirators Belle had reported

were already at Austin trying to discover what action
was contemplated to prevent a cure for the Texas fever
from being found.

When Freddie and Dusty were satisfied that what
they wanted to be known was passed on by Dell, they
passed a warning to Mark, who took over the next part
of the scheme by meeting Wax at Hereford. Having sur-
vived the two attempts upon his life and deducing who
Lance Sidcup and Amos Cruikshank really were—as
Dusty had when noticing the latter was eavesdropping
by lip-reading at the governor's reception in Austin—
Wax had set out to collect Frank Smith from Chicago.

From the moment the rusty-haired Texan left Hereford, the Kid, putting to use the training as a Comanche
warrior he had received as a boy, had followed him
without the men sent after him realizing that this was
taking place. When deciding that they had gone far
enough, the Kid had stolen their horses while they slept
and left the old pair of moccasins in the justified assumption that the oldest member of the party would
realize what this meant and also suspect his involvement.

The Kid had achieved his purpose and, satisfied that
there would by no further danger from that source, had
headed to the Smith ranch in Ellis County, where he
helped the Lombards ready its defenses in advance of
for Wax's arrival there. Not the least of these had been
the construction of the apparently solid mounds. In re-
ality these were domes of light sticks over which burlap
was spread and turf, brought from some distance away,
placed on top to be watered and tended until it started
to grow in a natural-looking manner. While this was
being carried out, in spite of the claim he had made
about having to "sage-hen" throughout the entire mission, he had stayed at the house, although taking the
precaution of wearing clothing less easily distinguish-
able than his usual all-black attire and making sure he

kept out of sight whenever anybody came visiting. By doing so, he had kept his presence in the area from being discovered. He felt the precaution was justified when news of the hard cases assembling in Waxahachie arrived and a couple of them carried out scouting forays to study the layout of the ranch house.

Notified by telegraph from Ashdown, Arkansas, that Wax would shortly reach Texas, the Kid had gone to the prearranged point for crossing the Red River. His sense of humor had demanded that he keep his presence from being discovered by any of the trio—although Wax formed the correct conclusion when the other two mentioned their belief that they were being watched by somebody they could not locate—yet remain ready to render assistance should the need arise. The attack on the house had come earlier than was anticipated. Nevertheless, so effective did the false mounds prove, it was broken up without the Kid's having needed to become involved until after the attackers were driven off. Trailing after them, he had prevented a return from being made and, as he discovered later, caused the survivors to decide to give up any further attempts.

After discussion over breakfast that morning, the Kid had had his proposal that the time had come to settle accounts with Steffen and his partner—if they could be found—accepted unanimously. Everybody agreed that there would be further attempts made against them as long as the pair were at liberty to do so. Wax and Teddy had gone to the Gunnison Hotel as the most likely place to find their quarry, and, on entering, found their assumption to be correct—at least as far as the Actor was concerned, for his partner had not been with him.

"I'm afraid you have the wrong man, my son," Walter Steffen claimed, although he realized from the use of the sobriquet "Actor" that the Texan confronting him was aware of his true identity. Moving his right hand

slowly, he unfastened the black jacket and, making a
scratching motion in a seemingly nonchalant fashion
with his fingers, slipped it underneath toward the waiting handle of the Merwin & Hulbert revolver. "Damn it,
I've picked up a flea!"

Making the second comment, the hired killer coiled
his hand around the butt of the revolver confident that
his true intention was not expected.

There was one thing that the Actor failed to take into
account due to his ignorance of certain vitally important
matters.

Despite having acquired reasonable skill at handling
revolvers, Steffen had done so east of the Mississippi
River. Nor had he ever seen a Western-trained *pistolero*
in action. He was not present when Waxahachie Smith
and Mark Counter dealt with their attackers in the dining room of the Hereford hotel. Furthermore, none of
the men whom he had hired rated as efficient gunfight-
ers. Therefore, he had nothing upon which to base his
assessment of the situation. Instead, despite having
been identified, he was confident that his intended victim was unaware that he was armed.

In the latter assumption, the Actor was completely
wrong.

For a good many years, Wax had been associated and
in contention with men well versed in all aspects of gunplay. Among the survival lessons he had learned was the
ability to watch for and locate hidden weapons. Scan-
ning Steffen while approaching, he had noticed the
bulge beneath the left side of the fastened jacket and
drawn the correct conclusion as to its cause. What was
more, pretending to scratch at a nonexistent flea was an
old ploy, even though Steffen believed he had just
thought it up. In fact, the rusty-haired Texan thought the
action gave added evidence to his estimate of the other
being armed.

Satisfied that he had lulled Wax's suspicions, the Ac-

tor grasped and started to twist the short-barreled revolver from the spring-retention shoulder holster.

With the move commenced, Steffen began to realize
that he had been wrong in his assessment of the situation.

Twisting palm outward, the rusty-haired Texan
brought his slip gun from its Missouri Skin-Tite holster
with a deft and deadly-flowing speed that bespoke long
practice. With the action cocked as the Colt emerged,
turned forward before the other man's weapon came
into view, flame and smoke erupted from the muzzle. At
such close quarters, even though the barrel was being
pointed at waist level by instinctive alignment, the
multi-ball load of the cartridge flew as intended. All
three pieces of lead plowed into the center of Steffen's
chest and, allowing the Merwin & Hulbert to slip from
his suddenly inoperative fingers, he toppled backward to
the floor.

As soon as Cruikshank saw his partner reaching beneath the jacket, he knew what to expect. Bringing out
his own weapon, he stepped forward and started to raise
it. Things might have gone badly for Teddy, as he had
forgotten there were two men to be found. Although he
glanced around and recognized the danger with which
he was being threatened, he could not react swiftly
enough to save himself. Nor, being occupied by dealing
with Steffen, was Wax in a better position to deal with
the second menace.

Thrusting himself across the threshold from where he
had remained to keep watch on his companions, the
Ysabel Kid brought his magnificent "One of a Thousand" Winchester Model of 1873 to his shoulder with
smooth-flowing rapidity. Hardly had the butt been cra-
dled at his right shoulder than the octagonal barrel was
aligned to his satisfaction and a squeeze at the set trigger caused the weapon to fire. Struck between the eyes
by the .44-caliber bullet, its director having concluded

that only such a means would serve to save Teddy, Cruikshank was killed instantly and driven backward a couple of involuntary paces to measure his length on the floor.

"Bully, Lon!" Teddy boomed, having watched his would-be assailant go down, then turned his gaze to the black-dressed, Indian-dark Texan. "And my thanks, sir. I owe you my life."

Stepping forward to kick the Merwin & Hulbert farther away from its owner, Wax studied the effect of his shot.

Although Steffen was still alive, the three segments of the multi-ball load formed a triangle in his chest to inflict a wound from which not even the best medical attention would have enabled him to survive.

"Why didn't you stop me if you knew who I was and what I was after?" the Actor croaked, looking upward.

"We concluded to make you spend a whole heap of those lib-rad sons of bitches' money before we called time on your game," Wax replied, knowing nothing could save the man and willing to do what little was possible to give relief for his remaining life span.

"Goddamn it!" Steffen growled, swinging his eyes to where Teddy was approaching. "You're the only one I ever failed to get once I started, Smith."

"He's not Frank Smith," Wax stated before his companion could speak.

"Not—?" the Actor gasped, but a spasm shook him to end the question unsaid.

"Nope," Wax confirmed when Steffen showed signs of being able to concentrate again. "Freddie and Dusty Fog fetched Frank back with them from Chicago, and he's been working on the cure for the Texas fever down to their spread in Rio Hondo County ever since."

"But why—?" the Actor croaked.

"To stop anybody finding out where he was and trying to stop him doing it," Wax explained. "And, like I said, make those softshells waste their money. I hope you soaked them *good.*"

"I—I did, much good it will do me now," Steffen admitted, then went on, "But if he isn't Frank Smith, who is he?"

"His real name's Theodore Roosevelt, but he'd sooner be called Teddy," Smith replied. "And even if he doesn't do anything else in his life, he's sure done a real service for the cattle business in Texas."

1. Walter "the Actor" Steffen had a son and grandson who took up his profession as a hired killer. While we have no information about the career of the former, we have recorded the fate of the latter in CAP FOG, TEXAS RANGER, MEET MR. J. G. REEDER.

APPENDIX

With his exceptional good looks and magnificent physical development,[1] Mark Counter presented the kind of appearance many people expected of a man with the reputation gained by his *amigo,* Captain Dustine Edward Marsden "Dusty" Fog. It was a fact of which they took advantage when the need arose.[2] On one occasion, it was also the cause of the blond giant being subjected to a murder attempt although the Rio Hondo gun wizard was the intended victim.[3]

While serving as a lieutenant under the command of General Bushrod Sheldon in the War Between the States, Mark's merits as an efficient and courageous officer had been overshadowed by his unconventional taste in uniforms. Always something of a dandy, coming from a wealthy family had allowed him to indulge in his whims. Despite considerable opposition and disapproval from hidebound senior officers, his adoption of a "skirtless" tunic in particular had come to be much copied by the other rich young bloods of the Confederate States Army.[4] Similarly, in later years, having received an independent income through the will of a maiden aunt,[5] his taste in attire had dictated what the well-dressed cowhand from Texas should wear to be in fashion.

When peace had come between the North and the South, Mark had accompanied Sheldon to fight for Emperor Maximilian in Mexico. There he had met Dusty Fog and the Ysabel Kid. On returning with them to Texas, he had received an offer to join the floating outfit of the OD Connected ranch. Knowing his two older brothers could help his father, Big Ranse, to run the family's R Over C ranch in the Big Bend country—and considering life would be more enjoyable and exciting in the company of his two *amigos*—he accepted.

An expert cowhand, Mark had become known as Dusty's right bower.[6] He had also gained acclaim by virtue of his enormous strength. Among other feats, it was told how he had used a tree trunk in the style of a Scottish caber to dislodge outlaws from a cabin in which they had forted up,[7] and broke the neck of a Texas longhorn steer with his bare hands.[8] He had acquired further fame for his ability at bare-handed roughhouse brawling. However, because he had spent so much time in the company of the Rio Hondo gun wizard, his full potential as a gunfighter received little attention. Nevertheless, men who were competent to judge such matters stated that he was second only to the small Texan when it came to drawing fast and shooting accurately with a brace of long barreled Colt revolvers.[9]

Many women found Mark irresistible, including Martha "Calamity

Jane" Canary.[10] However, in his younger days, only one—the lady
outlaw, Belle Starr—held his heart.[11] It was not until several years
after her death that he courted and married Dawn Sutherland, whom
he had first met on the trail drive taken by Colonel Charles Goodnight
to Fort Sumner, New Mexico.[12] The discovery of oil on their ranch
brought added wealth to them, and this commodity now forms the
major part of the present family's income.[13]

Recent biographical details we have received from the current head
of the family, Andrew Mark "Big Andy" Counter, establish that Mark
was descended on his mother's side from Sir Reginald Front de Boeuf,
notorious as lord of Torquilstone Castle in medieval England[14] and
who lived up to the family motto, *Cave Adsum*.[15] However, although a
maternal aunt and her son, Jessica and Trudeau Front de Boeuf, behaved in a way that suggested they had done so,[16] the blond giant had
not inherited the very unsavory character and behavior of his ancestor.

*1. Two of Mark Counter's grandsons, Andrew Mark "Big Andy" Counter
and Ranse Smith inherited his good looks and exceptional physique as
did two great-grandsons, Deputy Sheriff Bradford "Brad" Counter and
James Allenvale "Bunduki" Gunn. Unfortunately, while willing to supply
information about other members of his family, past and present, "Big
Andy" has so far declined to allow publication of any of his own adven-
tures.*
*1a. Some details of Ranse Smith's career as a peace officer during the
Prohibition Era are recorded in:* THE JUSTICE OF COMPANY "Z,"
THE RETURN OF RAPIDO CLINT AND MR. J. G. REEDER,
and RAPIDO CLINT STRIKES BACK.
1b. Brad Counter's activities are described in: Part Eleven, "Preventive
Law Enforcement," J.T.'S HUNDREDTH *and the Rockabye County
series, covering aspects of law enforcement in present day Texas.*
1c. Some of James Gunn's life story is told in: Part Twelve, "The
Mohawi's Powers," J.T.'s HUNDREDTH *and the Bunduki series. His
nickname arose from the Swahili word for a handheld firearm of any
kind,* "bunduki," *and gave rise to the horrible pun that when he was a
child he was,* "toto ya bunduki," *meaning, "son of a gun."*
2. One occasion is recorded in: THE SOUTH WILL RISE AGAIN.
*2a. Information about the career and special abilities of Captain Dustine
Edward Marsden "Dusty" Fog can be found in various volumes of the
Civil War and Floating Outfit series.*
3. The incident is described in: BEGUINAGE.
4. The Manual of Dress Regulations *for the Confederate States Army
stipulated that the tunic should have "a skirt extending halfway between
hip and knee."*
5. The legacy also caused two attempts to be made upon Mark's life, see:

CUT ONE, THEY ALL BLEED *and* Part Two, "We Hang Horse Thieves High," J.T.'S HUNDREDTH.

6. "Right bower"; second in command, derived from the name given to the second highest trump card in the game of euchre.

7. Told in: RANGELAND HERCULES.

8. Told in: THE MAN FROM TEXAS, *this is a rather "pin the tail on the donkey" title used by our first publishers to replace our own,* ROUNDUP CAPTAIN, *which we considered far more apt.*

9. Evidence of Mark Counter's competence as a gunfighter and his standing compared to Dusty Fog is given in: GUN WIZARD.

10. Martha "Calamity Jane" Canary's meetings with Mark Counter are described in: Part One, "The Bounty on Belle Starr's Scalp," TROUBLED RANGE; *its "expansion,"* TEXAS TRIO, Part One, "Better than Calamity," THE WILDCATS; *its "expansion,"* CUT ONE, THEY ALL BLEED; THE BAD BUNCH; THE FORTUNE HUNTERS; THE BIG HUNT *and* GUNS IN THE NIGHT.

10a. Further details about the career of Martha Jane Canary are given in the Calamity Jane *series, also;* Part Seven, "Deadwood, August the 2nd, 1876"; J.T.'S HUNDREDTH; Part Six, "Mrs. Wild Bill," J.T.'S LADIES *and she makes a "guest" appearance in,* Part Two, "A Wife for Dusty Fog," THE SMALL TEXAN.

11. How Mark Counter's romance with Belle Starr commenced, progressed, and ended is told in: Part One, "The Bounty on Belle Starr's Scalp," TROUBLED RANGE; *its "expansion,"* TEXAS TRIO; THE BAD BUNCH; RANGELAND HERCULES; THE CODE OF DUSTY FOG; Part Two, "We Hang Horse Thieves High," J.T.'S HUNDREDTH; THE GENTLE GIANT; Part Four, "A Lady Known as Belle," THE HARD RIDERS *and* GUNS IN THE NIGHT.

11a. Belle Starr "stars"—no pun intended—in: CARDS AND COLTS; Part Four, "Draw Poker's Such a *Simple* Game," J.T.'S LADIES RIDE AGAIN *and* WANTED! BELLE STARR.

11b. She also makes "guest" appearances in: THE QUEST FOR BOWIE'S BLADE; Part One, "The Set-up," SAGEBRUSH SLEUTH; *its "expansion,"* WACO'S BADGE *and* Part Six, "Mrs. Wild Bill," J.T.'S LADIES.

11c. We are frequently asked why it is the "Belle Starr" we describe is so different from a photograph which appears in various books. The research of the world's foremost fictionist genealogist, Philip Jose Farmer— author of, among numerous other works, TARZAN ALIVE: A DEFINITIVE BIOGRAPHY OF LORD GREYSTOKE *and* DOC SAVAGE: HIS APOCALYPTIC LIFE—*with whom we consulted have established the lady about whom we are writing is not the same person as another equally famous bearer of the name. However, the Counter family have asked Mr. Farmer and ourselves to keep her true identity a secret and this we intend to do.*

12. Told in: GOODNIGHT'S DREAM *and* FROM HIDE AND HORN.

13. This is established by inference in: Case Three, "The Deadly Ghost," ALVIN FOG, TEXAS RANGER.

14. See: IVANHOE, *by Sir Walter Scott.*

15. "Cave Adsum"; roughly translated from Latin, "Beware, I am Here."

16. Some information about Jessica and Trudeau Front de Boeuf can be found in: CUT ONE, THEY ALL BLEED; Part Three, "Responsibility to Kinfolks," OLE DEVIL'S HANDS AND FEET *and* Part Four, "The Penalty of False Arrest," MARK COUNTER'S KIN.